KING II

Jimmy DaSaint

KING II

Published by DASAINT ENTERTAINMENT
Po Box 97 Bala Cynwyd, PA 19004
Website: www.dasaintentertainment.com

"Nearly all men can stand adversity, but if you want to test a man's character, give him power."

-Abraham Lincoln

The tongue is a small thing, but what enormous damage it can do.

-James 3:5

Chapter 1
Two Months Later

After eight grueling weeks of multiple operations and rehabilitation, King was starting to regain his strength. The two bullets that lacerated his stomach were life threatening, but through the grace of God, he managed to pull through. When King returned home from the hospital, he hired a personal nurse to help with rehab, give him his meds, and monitor his day-to-day status. King's wife, Queen, begged him to let her help at work with Zeta and Biggie until he was healthy enough to return. After a week of trying to convince him, King finally gave in.

For three long days, King gave Queen all the jewels and knowledge of the business, and he even taught her about the corruption in the brutal drug game. He was surprised at how quickly she picked it all up including her knowledge of the streets. So, throughout the day Queen would be out handling business by herself or with Biggie, and at night she would be back at home in their Wynnewood Estate taking care of her wounded husband.

They all knew they were involved in a brutal and violent drug war with Vance and his ruthless organization. In the past two months, three men from both sides had been murdered in cold blood, causing the war to escalate to the highest it has been since Face passed the throne to King. No one on the street was safe, and everyone was a target.
The Philadelphia PD Commissioner and the Philadelphia District Attorney's office assembled a special taskforce to take both sides down. With dozens of informants all over the city, gathering vital information, the DA's office was sure to get Grand Jury indictments on members of both sides. Now

there was a new player in the game, and her name was District Attorney Candice Shaw.

58th Street, Southwest Philly

Victor, Natasha, Terry, and Rosa stood around and watched as Vance peeled the bandage from the wound on his neck. Luckily, the bullet that entered his neck missed his main artery by a mere centimeter. If the bullet had hit the artery, it would've surely stopped the blood supply to his brain and Vance would have died in moments.

"Finally, I can take this shit off," Vance said in a strained voice. "Now it's time to get back to business and run that punk ass King out of Philly."

"What about your daughter Queen? I heard she is helping them now," Terry asked.

Vance stood up and paced the floor before saying, "I will take care of Queen. Any new info?"

"After my cousin, Tito was busted by the Feds I had to get us a new connect from Colombia," Rosa said.

Vance just nodded his head. Unbeknown to everyone, Vance had been the person responsible for helping the Feds indict and arrest Tito. Like most of the people that Vance helped to put behind bars, he too had once pleaded out of a 40-year sentence in federal prison.

"Did Tito say anything about his case?" Vance asked curiously. "No, when I went to visit him he seemed very scared. I've never seen him like that before. He lost so much weight, and he don't look the same. The Feds broke him and most of his organization."

"Who is the new contact?" Vance asked. "It's a guy named Paco. He is Tito's uncle from Bogota, Colombia. Much bigger and more ruthless than Tito."

Vance smiled and said, “Set up a meeting ASAP.”
“Anything else?”
“Yeah, we found out about a new dope house that King got out in West Philly,” Terry said. “Okay then, you and Victor can go handle that. That bitch ass nigga will not make a dime in my city,” Vance laughed.

Chapter 2
Chester, PA

Inside a large private warehouse, Queen and Zeta were sitting at a table separating 300 kilos of cocaine. The new shipment had just been dropped off, and now it was time to flood the streets with the product. As Queen separated the drugs a message from Biggie appeared on her phone. After reading it, she asked Zeta to follow her into a small black office.

"Wassup?" Zeta asked. "Biggie brought the two guys with him that he wanted us to meet."

Moments later, Biggie walked in with two men and introduced them. "This is my good friend Black Gotti and his partner, Marvin. They have been secretly working with our team for a while now. Gotti and Marvin grew up with King and me. They are from our West Philly neighborhood. Real stand up men." Biggie said, confidently.

"I heard about y'all," Zeta said. "And if it's all true I'm glad to have y'all be a part of the team."

Queen stood there staring into Gotti's eyes and eyeing both of them down. Both men were handsome with calm demeanors.

"So why do they call you Black Gotti?" she asked.

"Because I'm half Black and half Italian and I have a low tolerance for snitches, cops, and people's bullshit," he replied. Queen smiled and asked, "What about you?"

"Ditto," Marvin said.

"So, what have y'all been doing for us?"

Gotti laughed and looked over at Biggie and said, "Do you want me to tell her?"

"You can tell her," Biggie replied.

"Well, you know about the three men that were recently kidnapped and murdered from Vance's crew?"
"Yeah, what about them?" Queen asked.
"That was our work. We are also the ones that blew up Vance's daycares and food trucks. We also..."
"Okay, I get it," Queen said. "I want to bring you in more. You were our ears and eyes on the streets. Feared and respected."

Queen walked up to Gotti and looked straight into his eyes. "What about loyalty?"
Without hesitation, Gotti said, "I'd rather die than cross my team. And I'd rather sit in a cell before I tell."

Queen could tell that Gotti meant what he said. His eyes told the truth, and she could feel them penetrating her skin. She knew that the two handsome men were also cold-blooded killers, and they would be assets in King's organization.

"So, what do y'all need?" she asked.
"More guns. More coke and a few untraceable cell phones. Tell us what you want back and you will have it on time. Tell us who you want dead and we will bring you back the obituary," Gotti said in a serious tone.
"Can you handle 50 kilos at 18 Grand apiece?" Queen asked.
"Why not, just let me know when you need the $900 Grand," Gotti answered with a smirk.

Queen shook both of their hands and said, "Welcome to the team. A shipment of 50 kilos, four AK-47's, four 9mm handguns, two bullet proof vests and two untraceable cell phones will be dropped off at 5 pm at the location of your choice."

Gotti and Marvin pleasingly shook their heads and followed Biggie out the door.

"What do you think Zeta?"
"Well, besides both of them being drop dead gorgeous they have a rep out in Philly for being some cold-blooded killers that don't play with anyone! I hear Gotti's father is a made member in the Philly Italian Mob. Plus, they are both loyal," she replied.

"I like them, plus I can tell they are serious about what they do for work. If I wasn't married I would turn that sexy motherfucker out!" Queen laughed.

Zeta laughed as well and said, "As long as I can join in."

When the laughter ended Queen and Zeta walked back into the room filled with piles of cocaine. It was worth over $3 million dollars on the streets, and the streets were patiently waiting.

Chapter 3
Later That Evening

At the Marriott Hotel on City Line Avenue, Vance was inside a room talking with two FBI agents. Agents Tony and Lucas had been assigned to Vance's case for almost twenty years. For over a decade Vance had been their number one street informant. In the past twenty years, Vance was personally responsible for over 200 arrests and convictions. His FBI file was confidential with other high-profile informants, witnesses, and top criminals. As long as Vance got the Feds major players and large drug and weapons seizures, he was allowed to run his drug organization with no interference from the FBI or DEA.

Vance was a pawn in the government's chess game, just like Sammy "The Bull" Gravano, Joseph Valachi, Joseph Massino, and Henry Hill. Vance had been the FBI's ears and eyes for the entire tri-state area. But now his daughter and his enemy, King, had discovered his deep dark secret. Vance needed them both dead before they had the chance to expose him, so his team of hit men had been vigorously searching for them.

In the meantime, Vance continued to work with his friends at the FBI to help bring drug dealers, Philly Mafia members, and murderers to justice. He was a cop without a badge, being protected and paid by the Feds to ignore the code of the streets.

"So, what's the good news you got for us?" Agent Lucas asked.

With a huge smile on his face, Vance said, "I got a big fish! I can get you Paco Vazquez. One of the top men of the Bloque Meta Cartel in Colombia."

Both agents' eyes lit up with excitement. "A bust like Paco will get us both promotions in the Bureau," Agent Tony said. "He's been on the FBI's 10 Most Wanted List for seven years!"

"Are you sure?" Agent Lucas asked. "I'm positive. He's related to Rosa. After we took Tito down, he has been her supplier for New York, Philly, AC, Camden, Boston, Baltimore, and DC." Vance replied.

"Well, we can just take Rosa down and get her to turn on Paco. We have gathered a lot of damaging info on her since she started working with you," Agent Tony said.

"No, I'm not ready to take Rosa down. She has been a major player in my game. I still need her out here, not in a Federal prison or the Witness Protection Program. She will help us get Paco and then y'all can take them down together. But I want to be paid for this one," Vance said.

"And you will Vance. You get us Paco Vazquez, and I'll personally send you a million dollars to your private offshore account in the Caymans," Agent Lucas said.

"What's up with King and his crew?" Agent Tony said, changing the subject. "He's still hiding, but don't y'all worry. I'm going to find out where he is soon, and when I do he is a dead man." Everyone stood around laughing.

After Vance had left the hotel room, he went outside and got into a waiting tinted black Mercedes Benz. "Wassup Vance? Did everything go well with your meeting with the real estate investors?" Rosa asked.

Vance smiled and nodded his head. "Yes, everything went well."

"Good, I'm trying to invest some more money into the Philly real estate market," Rosa said, before pulling off.

"So, when can you set up a meeting with Paco?" Vance asked.

"As soon as possible. I will call him later tonight," Rosa replied. As she continued to talk about Paco and other major criminals, she had no idea that every word was secretly being recorded.

Chapter 4
Wynnewood, PA

While King laid on the bed watching TV, Queen was across the room on the computer. For the past hour, she had been researching any and everything she could find out about her father. She had gotten some help from a member of King's crew named Roscoe, who was a professional computer hacker. Roscoe had shown Queen how to break into computer systems to find special information about certain individuals. Roscoe also installed special malware software that could disable computer systems.

"Did you find out anything about that snitch ass daddy of yours?" King asked. Queen stood from the chair and walked over to the bed and sat beside King.

"First of all, you're my only Daddy," she said, before kissing his cheek. "But no, the Feds must have his secret files locked away in a vault somewhere. I can't find anything on him. But what I did find out is that everyone he has worked with in the past has been arrested, convicted and serving up to 30 years or life sentences. A few of them have mysteriously died in prison. I believe that my father is responsible for putting them all away in Federal Penitentiaries. Ever since I was a little girl, I could remember him meeting up with those two agents. I could never forget their faces."

"Damn!" King said, shaking his head in disgust. "That's fucked up!"

"I'm gonna print out a list of all my father's former associates. For twenty years people have been getting set up and sent to the Feds by him. He's pathetic!" Queen said. "Roscoe is helping me gather more info."

King nodded his head and said, “We need to eliminate Vance! We can’t have a rat like that out here doing what he’s doing. I want you to get all the info you can on Vance so we can expose this rat to the whole city!”

“The whole world ... the whole world, “Queen said before she joined King in bed and laid across his chest. “Kill the rat,” she said.

Chapter 5
12:52 AM
West Philly
44th & Lancaster Avenue

Victor and Terry sat inside a white van. Behind the wheel was Victor's younger sister, Natasha. They had been parked for almost 45 minutes, patiently watching King's $20,000 a day dope house being flooded with traffic. People were going in and out of the large two-story building. A police car had driven past them twice, but behind the wheel was John Carter, a crooked cop that was on Vance's payroll. He was there to make sure nothing went wrong.

With two Molotov cocktails a piece, Victor and Terry got out of the van and walked towards the dope house. The sky was pitched black, and no one on the block paid them any attention. Victor watched as Terry walked through an alley and headed towards the back of the house.

At 12:55 AM Terry lit the wickers and threw both Molotov cocktails into the house. At the same time, Victor did the same. As they both walked away and got back into the van, they heard the large explosion and saw fire overtake the house. Some people were on fire as they were running out of the house and screaming for help. Natasha slowly pulled off with a smile on her face. "Vance will be happy for this," she said.

An hour later, firefighters were putting out the large fire and pulling out nine burnt bodies. Four of King's best workers and five of their friends had been savagely murdered inside the house. The local news had swarmed all over the block, and a large crowd of sad onlookers stood behind the police barricades in total shock. This had been one of the worst tragedies since the Lex Street Massacres in

December of 2000. Now once again this West Philly neighborhood had been stricken with violence and a new list of unsolved murders.

3:15 AM

As he laid in bed King could feel a wet substance on his leg. He quickly sat up and turned on the bed lamp. Queen instantly woke from her sleep and the first thing she noticed was that she was lying in a pool of blood.

"Oh shit!" she yelled.

King quickly helped her out of bed, watching as thick red blood dripped from her vagina. He rushed her into the bathroom and put her in the tub. Then he started to run warm water over her body. Queen lay there crying and shaking her head.

"No! No! No!" she cried out in total disbelief. Forty minutes later, they were at the local hospital receiving the worst news ever. Queen had a miscarriage after just a few months of pregnancy.

A few hours later, they were walking out of the hospital in dead silence. Queen had refused to stay overnight. She wanted to go home with her husband. When they finally reached home, King and Queen sat on the couch, and he cradled her in his arms. For a moment, there was an eerie silence. They had both wanted a child, and that dream had turned into a bloody nightmare.

Queen looked deep into King's watery eyes and wiped away his tears. "Don't worry, Daddy, we will have our baby one day. We are both strong; nothing can break us," she said, kissing him softly on the lips. "I'm going to rest for a day or two then it's back to business."

"Are you sure?" King asked.

"I'm positive, we got business to take care off," Queen replied, as they sat on the couch crying together. Neither one of them said another word.

Chapter 6
Early the Next Morning
Downtown Philadelphia

Candice Shaw was fuming with anger and total disbelief. The Philly drug war was getting way out of control. The Mayor and Governor had told her to "get it fixed by any means necessary."

Candice Shaw was a hard-nosed prosecutor and a woman who was determined to excel in her career. At just 5 feet 4 she stood like a tower when it came to her peers and the laws she enforced.

Inside her office, Candice sat among a group of men that were a part of a new drug task force. She had assembled the five-member group of law enforcers to help find and take down all the major drug dealers in the city. For weeks, they had been active in covert missions to gather info on different drug organizations. So far, their only major assets were street informants.

"Why does the name Vance Lewis continue to come up but we have yet to get one shred of information on him? How is it that this known killer and drug dealer has a blank record in our police database, and why won't the Feds help us out on this case?" Candice asked.

"I think they are hiding something on him that they don't want to get exposed," one of the officers said.

"Well Feds or not, if we can get something on Vance Lewis his ass is going down!" Candice said. "I'm going over to the FBI office to see what I can find out on Mr. Vance Lewis. Something just isn't right."

"Well, we are now gathering some info on Darius 'King' Smith, Rosa Gomez, Simon 'Black Gotti' Carter and a few others. We just need more info and informants that are willing to testify and help take them down," another officer replied.

Candice Shaw just sat there and smirked. "Good luck with that," she said, before ending the meeting.

West Philly
36th & Haverford Avenue

John Carter pulled up and parked his police car in front of a small house. Two Black men were standing outside waiting for his arrival. When the trunk popped open one of the men ran over and took out a Nike sports bag. Inside the bag was ten kilos of cocaine. The man grabbed the bag and ran into the house, while the other man got inside the police car.

"What's up John?" he said, as they shook hands. "I'm good Krack. That's the ten kilos you said you needed. Do you have the money? I have four more runs to make for Vance," John Carter said.

Krack reached inside his coat and took out a large plastic bag filled with cash. "It's all there. See you next week." Before Krack got out of the car, John reached over and grabbed his arm. "Are you okay? Did you take a break from the bottle?"

"I'm good, John, I stopped drinking after Vance gave me my job back, thanks for asking." After shaking hands, Krack watched as John drove off, headed for his next destination.

When Krack walked back into the house, two men were sitting in the living room waiting for him. Ten kilos were scattered on a long glass table. Also on the table was two bottles of Jack Daniels whiskey and an ounce of marijuana.

Lenny "Krack" Roberts was a top lieutenant in Vance's drug organization. He was one of his most loyal men. For three years Krack had been running the West Philly distribution for Vance's drug network. Vance's only problem with Krack was that he was addicted to the bottle. Not a day went by when Krack didn't get drunk. Money, women, and whiskey were what he lived for.

Chapter 7
56th & Chester Avenue
Southwest Philly

Plex was fuming with anger when he found out that Vance was still alive. He had shot him right outside of his window. He was positive that it was a kill shot. He planned every move like it was a chess game, but even so, he still didn't get the checkmate he wanted. Vance was the man responsible for his wife's brutal kidnapping and murder. For that Plex was determined to kill him, no matter how long it took.

As he sat there venting out his anger to his friend Bobby and a few others, Plex had no idea that someone in his circle was a snake, an opportunist looking for a major payday.

Baltimore, MD

After the attempted murder of King, Sofie left Philly and ran to B-More to live with her sister. She heard that King had somehow survived the two bullets he took in his stomach. King being alive put great fear into her soul, and she knew that Queen would one day come looking for her. Queen had a dark side to her that not many knew about, but Sofie was one of the few that knew all too well.

As Sofie sat on the sofa watching TV, she placed her hands on her plump stomach and began to rub it. The baby boy inside of her was growing fast. Sofie lied to Queen and never got an abortion. Her confused mind would not allow her to go through with it. For months Sofie had been confused and on edge, but as she sat there rubbing her belly, she could feel a wonderful sensation from the new life forming inside her.

"Just a few more months to go baby boy, and you and mommy will be together," Sofie said to herself. Still, all she could think about was Queen as the flow of tears fell from her eyes.

Chapter 8
23rd & Diamond Street
North Philly

"His name is Magic, and I'm telling you, Vance, this guy is a beast!" Terry said after he parked the car and they got out.

"But is he loyal?" Vance asked as they walked over to a small row house.

"This guy killed a man with his bare hands, and he is one of the most loyal dudes I know," Terry said excitedly.

Vance nodded his head. He knew that Terry was a good judge of character, especially when it came to people of loyalty.

After knocking on the door, they were greeted by a 6 ft. 5-inch giant. Magic was a dark-skinned man with a clean-shaven head. He weighed around 300 pounds and was all muscle. Terry and Vance walked into the house, and the first thing they noticed was an older woman and a teenage boy sitting in a wheelchair.

"Momma, can you take Simon into the other room? I need to talk to my friends," Magic said. After his mother had pushed the boy into another room, everyone took a seat on the sofa.

"I heard a lot of good things about you Magic," Vance said. "Thanks. I heard some good things about you as well. Your name rings bells up in the pen."

"Where did you do time at?" Vance asked, curiously. "I just finished up an eight-year bid at Gratersford for a manslaughter charge," Magic replied proudly. "Did Terry explain to you what we need from you?"

"Yes, muscle and loyalty. Plus, I know that you're in a war with the King crew. Fuck King and his crew! That nigga Biggie killed my cousin!!!" Magic vented.

Vance nodded his head and said, "Well if you roll with us I will help you get your revenge on that little midget bastard." After talking a little while longer, Vance asked, "So what's wrong with your little brother?"

"He has multiple sclerosis," Magic sadly replied. "That's my heart," he added.

Magic walked Terry and Vance to the door and watched as they walked over to the car and drove off. He couldn't wait to show Vance and Terry how loyal he was going to be to his new crew.

One week later, Wynnewood, PA

"I just got off the phone with my main connect and since I can't meet him myself, I'm gonna need y'all two to go down to Texas and meet with him for me," King told Biggie and Zeta.

"Okay, we on the first flight out of Philly, just set it up," Biggie replied.

"I would like to go too," Queen asked.

"Naw baby, I need you here with me. Plus, we still need to take care of that house fire situation where four of my men were killed." King said.

"Baby, I already got Gotti and Marvin taking care of that. They already found out that it was Vance's people behind the whole thing, and that his Russian hit man and his sister were seen down the street from the house that night," Queen said.

After Queen pleaded her case, King finally decided to let her go in place of Zeta. Zeta didn't have a problem not going; she would rather stay in Philly, running the day-today operations while King was still recuperating from his gunshot wounds. As for Queen, she wanted to know everything about how the drug distribution business really worked. She was almost obsessed with knowing. Her love for King was undeniable. She was in love with her husband, and there was nothing she wouldn't do for him. Unlike her father Vance, loyalty was a must.

Once King made the calls and set everything up with the connect, Queen started packing for the trip.

"Are you sure you want to do this?" King asked as he lay back on the bed.

Queen walked over and sat down beside him. "Baby you're still not well, and it's my job to hold you down no matter what it takes or what consequences I must face. I love you, Daddy, just trust me," she said.

Chapter 9
Two Days Later

Gotti and his right-hand man Marvin was out cruising the streets on a serious murder mission. Queen had given them the order to kill anyone that was associated with her father's organization.

Driving around inside a tinted black Impala there was a secret stash spot under the seat full of weapons and ammunition... 9mms with infrared beams, silencers, Glocks, and so much more. Killing was their specialty, but being on the hunt for enemies was just as exciting.

Queen had given them a list of faces and names that she wanted eliminated. She had heard about or had known most of the men and women that worked for or with her father. Queen knew that Vance was out doing the same, and whoever got to the other first would regret it. After driving all over Southwest Philly Gotti and Marvin decided to go up to the Northeast.

It had taken some time, but Triad leader Chow-men Chan and Johnny Morino found out that Vance had been behind both of their brothers' murders. They both had placed a million-dollar bounty for anyone that gave them valid information leading to Vance's death. For months Vance was nowhere in sight, neither was anyone in his crew. They had been moving secretly and silently, avoiding authorities and enemies.

But Chow-men Chan and Johnny would not stop searching until Vance had reached the same fate as their brothers. With the word about the million-dollar bounty all over the streets, people were talking. Chow and Johnny each knew that it was just a matter of time until someone came to them with the right information.

Chapter 10
Pennsauken, New Jersey

"My cousin will be here on Thursday to meet you. I put in a good word for you and told him that you were Tito's biggest cocaine buyer and distributor for Philly, Camden, Delaware and Atlantic City. He's looking forward to the meeting," Rosa said to Vance.

"Thanks, I can't wait. Paco Vazquez is major. With him we can take over the entire city and beyond," Vance said enthusiastically.

"Did you find out anything new about my daughter?" Vance said, changing the subject.

"I did hear that she is helping King run things on the streets. King was badly shot a few months ago is what I'm hearing, so Queen is in charge now," Rosa said.

"Is that true?" Vance asked, surprised.

"That's the word on the streets."

"That no good bitch! I can't believe she crossed me like that!" Vance vented. "She knows too much about me, about most of my crew. That's why I had to relocate and distance myself. She needs to go ASAP!"

Rosa stood up from her chair and said, "What happened between you two? Why did things go haywire between you and your daughter?"

"It's a long story. It has something to do with her mother's death. She blamed me," Vance said, as his cell phone started to ring.

"What is it, Terry? Are you sure? Okay, I'm on my way down there now. Make sure everything is secure," he said before ending the call.

"What's wrong?" Rosa asked.

"Somebody has news about who shot me. They want to meet me at my bar on Ridge Avenue."

"I thought it was King and Queen."

"I did too, but I want to listen to all this guy has to say," Vance said before he and Rosa left the house.

Chapter 11
Tuesday Night
Oxford Circle, Northeast Philly

Gotti and Marvin sat in their car that was parked in the Checkers restaurant parking lot. While they were enjoying their burgers and fries, they noticed a familiar face at the McDonald's restaurant on the other side of the Circle. The tall, attractive white woman was a person that they had known too well. It was Natasha Gavrikov, Victor Gavrikov's younger sister, a cold-blooded female assassin who worked for Vance. They looked at the small photo Queen had given them to use to identify Natasha. It was definitely her.

They watched as Natasha got out of a red Ford Taurus and walked toward the restaurant. Today had been their lucky day Gotti thought to himself. Gotti and Marvin both put on their black ski masks and grabbed their loaded 9 mms. Silencers were attached to each one. Marvin pulled the Impala around and parked behind Natasha's Ford.

Moments later, they both watched as Natasha walked out of McDonald's holding two bags of food. As soon as she approached her car both men bounced out of the car with guns aimed and blazing. Natasha was caught completely off-guard and didn't stand a chance.

POW! POW! POW! POW! Gotti and Marvin unloaded every single bullet in their clips. They watched as Natasha fell hard to the cold ground, still holding both bags in her lifeless hands. It happened so fast and quiet that no one heard or saw a thing. Gotti then took out his cell phone and snapped a picture of Natasha's dead body.

Within seconds, Gotti and Marvin were driving down Roosevelt Boulevard, headed back to West Philly. With one name off the list now, there were just a few more to go.

"That's what they get for blowing up the house and killing our homies," Gotti said.

Chapter 12
Inside a small back room at the Ridge Capital Bar Ridge Avenue

Vance, Victor, Terry, and Rosa stood circled around the tall, slim nervous man listening as he spilled his guts about the hatched murder plot to kill Vance. The man's name was Anthony, and he had been a close friend to Plex and Bobby. At the present time, Anthony was dead broke, and he needed money to get a fix for his drug habit. For years, he had been addicted to heroin, crack, and marijuana.

"So, you're telling me that Queen and King had nothing to do with me getting shot?" Vance asked.

"I don't think so. Plex had been plotting to kill you and your crew for weeks, and he never mentioned anything about King or Queen. He only talked about avenging his wife's death," Anthony said.

"So, what is it that you want?" Vance asked.

"I figured for the info I gave you that it should be at least worth about $100,000. Plus, I can tell y'all where they be at."

"Where?" Terry asked.

"Not until I get paid," Anthony said.

"Pay him," Vance told Terry.

Terry placed a black briefcase on the table and opened it. Stacked neatly inside was $300,000 in cash. Terry counted out $100,000 and passed it to Anthony. His eyes widened with excitement, and he couldn't believe his underhanded plan worked. Anthony didn't care about anyone but himself. As long as he could get some money for his drug habit, he didn't care about the consequences of his actions. Anthony was the friend that kept a fake smile on his face but real jealousy and hate in his heart.

"Let's go, I'm going to ride with you," Terry said.

"Okay," Anthony said, as he put his money inside his pocket.

Moments later, Anthony was driving off with Vance, Victor and Rosa tailing closely behind them. They were all headed to Southwest Philly, where Plex and Bobby had no idea that the murder team was coming.

Chapter 13
El Paso, TX

El Paso is a city situated on the far western corner of Texas, right on the Mexican border. It stands on the Rio Grande, across the border from Ciudad Juarez, Chihuahua, Mexico. Not too far from the Fort Bliss military complex. Queen, Biggie, and two short Mexican men were in a small home. Juan Carlos and his younger cousin Arturo Salazar were two of the top members of the notorious Los Zetas Drug Cartel. They were King's new drug suppliers, introduced to them by King's older cousin Face.

"We can provide your organization with 1,000 to 2,000 kilos every two months, at a wholesale price of $12,000 a kilo," Juan said. Biggie and Queen just sat back and observed.

Dressed in an all-black body suit that accentuated her perfect hour-glass figure, Queen could see the lust in both men's eyes as they eyed her from head to toe. She knew that her full breasts and fat, plump ass could stop any man dead in their tracks. Queen had the demeanor as a female boss with the face and body of a video vixen. Her full lips and sexy eyes had them both star struck, and the scent of her Chanel No-5 had them almost hypnotized.

Queen stood up from her chair and walked over to both men. They had never seen a tall, exotic, aggressive black woman like Queen before.

"How about we negotiate the price and the kilo amount. First, we have over 100 local and national distributors for your product. Second, I personally guarantee a safe delivery at an undisclosed, private location. Third, if you supply us with between 2,000 and 4,000 kilos a month we will become your number one cocaine, heroin and marijuana distributors on the entire East Coast." Queen said, as she touched Arturo's shoulder and licked her pink lips.

Queen then worked her way over to Juan and ran her fingers through his dark, curly hair. She could see the excitement growing in his jeans. Biggie sat back in awe of the whole situation. He watched as Queen put on an Oscar winning performance. She had both men melting in her manicured fingers.

"So how about $9,000 a kilo and we start off with 3,000 of them?" Queen said as she sat down on Juan Carlo's lap. "That's twenty-seven million dollars, and I can guarantee that you will have it shipped to wherever you want in six weeks," Queen said, as she stood up and walked back over to Biggie and sat back down.

"Give us one minute," Juan said in his broken English. Queen and Biggie watched as the two men stood up and stepped away. They could hear them discussing something in Spanish.

Moments later, they walked back over to the table and Arturo said, "You're very good with your persuasion, so good that we are both convinced to trust and believe everything you said, Queen. It's a deal." Queen smiled, trying not to show the enthusiasm that filled her body.

Biggie just sat there silent and shocked. He had just watched Queen seduce two Mexican drug bosses into agreeing to deliver them the biggest drug shipment that King ever had, with a wholesale price that was sure to eliminate all the competition.

After getting all the proper details, distribution drop off spots and other keynotes Queen said, "Okay fellas, dinner is on me, I'm starving. I hear there are some very nice Mexican restaurants here in El Paso." Moments later, they were all inside Juan Carlos' Mercedes-Maybach S600, laughing, drinking champagne and heading towards the Carnitas Queretaro restaurant.

Chapter 14
58th & Woodland Avenue
Southwest Philly

The two cars pulled up and parked across the street from a two-story building.
"They is in that building right there," Anthony pointed out. "Now I got to go."
"Hold up; first I need you to call Plex and tell him to open the door. Tell him that you are on your way in with some news about Vance's whereabouts," Terry told him.
Anthony did as he was told and made the call.
"Yo wassup, Ant?" Plex answered.
"I got some good news about where Vance is that you need to hear. Unlock the door; I will be there in a few minutes."
"Okay," Plex said, ending the call.
"It's done, now can I leave?" Anthony said. Drugs were calling his name, and he needed a fix fast.
With a loaded .40 caliber inside his jacket pocket, Terry quickly pulled it out and aimed it at Anthony's head.
"Hey man, please don't kill me, I gave you what you wanted!!" he begged.
"Fuck you, nigga!" Terry said before he pulled the trigger and blew a section of Anthony's brain on the window and steering wheel.

Terry quickly took all the money out of Anthony's pockets and rushed out of the car. Then he along with Victor, Vance and Rosa walked over to the building and rushed inside. Sitting on a sofa playing the X-Box was Plex and Bobby. They had been completely caught off guard. With guns from all angles pointed at them they sat there in total fear, with their hands raised high.

Vance walked over to Plex and said, "So you're the bitch ass nigga that shot me huh?"
"You killed my wife!!" Plex shouted.
"Well, now you can join the bitch!" Vance said, and everyone started shooting.

The scene was something out of a mob movie. Plex and Bobby had both been shot over 20 times in the head and body. Both men were dead. Their X-Box controllers were on their laps, and the Call of Duty game was still playing. Moments later, they were all headed back to the Northeast where some disturbing news would be waiting for them.

Chapter 15
Wednesday Night

Candice Shaw was incensed with all the murders that had been going on throughout the city. The Mayor and Governor of Pennsylvania were putting lots of pressure on the D.A.'s office. They both threatened to audit the entire D.A. office if things did not get any better.

In less than a year Philly had over 420 homicides, with most of them drug related. Once again, the city was the number one murder capital in the USA over Chicago and New Orleans. The special drug task force she had organized had yet to get a key informant or find some vital info that would help take a major drug kingpin off the streets. Candice knew she needed to step up quickly or she would risk being suspended. Still, she had no intentions of giving up. She was determined to use all her assets in law enforcement and take the violent Philly streets back.

Wynnewood, PA

"I still can't believe you got us a deal like that!" King said as he and Queen sat on the bed. "$9,000 a kilo is unbelievable! At that price, we will have the streets on lock for years. Nobody will be able to compete with us in Philly, nobody!" King said enthusiastically.

"I told you to just trust me and I got you, love," Queen said, as she began to pull down King's boxers. King just sat back shaking his head in total disbelief. He knew that Queen was like no other woman he had ever had. She was beauty, brains, and business all wrapped up in one.

Queen got up and turned off the light, then she got undressed and joined her husband in bed.

"Take it easy babe, you know I'm still healing from the gunshots," King told her.

"Just relax, I got this," Queen said as she settled in between King's long legs.

As King laid back, Queen started licking and sucking his long, thick, hard dick. She pleased King until he couldn't take it anymore. When he finally ejaculated, she swallowed every single drop of his come then watched King exhale and relax onto the bed.

"I told you, I got this," Queen smiled. "Now relax for a few until I get it back up. I'm sucking your dick all night Daddy."

Northeast Philly

"I'm going to kill everyone!!" Victor shouted.

Vance, Terry and Rosa stood around in disbelief. After hearing about Natasha's brutal death, they were all speechless and saddened. She was a major asset to the crew for a few years.

"Queen is behind this, I just know it," Vance vented. "She has seen you and your sister many times. She knows all of y'alls faces from seeing y'all over at my house. She told King everything," Vance said as he stood there fuming with anger.

"Don't worry Victor. They can't keep hiding, and when I do find them death will be waiting," Terry said.

Victor didn't say a word; he just stood there letting the tears fall from his eyes. Four years earlier his younger sister moved to America in search of a better life. She had come to the US to escape the crime, poverty, and violence in Moscow, Russia. Now she was dead, with over twenty bullets in her body.

Victor turned and walked out of the house.

"Let him go," Vance told Terry, who was about to follow him. "He needs to get whatever it is off of his chest."

Back inside his van Victor started it up and sped off down the street. Lying on the floor in the back of the van were two AK-47's and a small box of hand grenades.

"I'm going to kill them all, Natasha!" Victor shouted to himself. "Every last one of them!"

As Victor drove down Roosevelt Boulevard, headed to West Philly, all he could think about was seeing Natasha's bullet riddled body lying on a table in the morgue.

Chapter 16
Thursday Afternoon
Miami, FL

The Ritz Carlton Hotel was situated in the heart of Miami Beach. Collins Avenue was one of the richest and hottest spots in all of Miami. Inside a private room, Vance and Rosa had been patiently waiting for Paco Vazquez to arrive. He was an hour late, and they were both starting to worry.

Finally, the doorknob turned and in walked a short, stocky man with dark, curly hair and a full beard. Paco Vazquez was portraying himself as a legitimate businessman, here in America to purchase one million dollars in commercial real estate. Behind the façade, Paco was one of the biggest drug dealers in the world. For the past year, he had been using his political and underground connections to slip in and out of the country.

"What took you so long?" Rosa asked, as Paco walked over and took a seat.

"I had to meet up with a few friends," Paco replied.

"This is my friend Vance. He was working with Tito before he got arrested by the Feds."

Paco and Vance shook hands.

"This is a nice spot," Vance said.

"Thank you; it is co-owned by one of my close friends. That's why I chose it," Paco said. "I have many friends located all throughout Miami and the Caribbean Islands."

Rosa interrupted and said, "Vance is a major player on the East Coast, and since Tito is gone now Vance could be an asset for us. I can't do it alone."

As they continued to talk about the East Coast drug distribution, the entire room was bugged and under heavy video surveillance. They had all been secretly tracked and followed by the DEA and FBI. With a big smile, Vance relaxed and let Paco and Rosa do all the talking.

Chapter 17
42nd and Mantua
West Philly

"Damn, y'all lit that Russian bitch the fuck up!!" Biggie said to Gotti and Marvin. "That shit was overkill!"

Gotti passed Biggie a large, black Nike sports bag and said, "It's all about leaving a message. I knew y'all would like the picture I sent," he smiled.

"So, what's next?" Biggie said.

"We on a serious mission Biggie. We out here on the streets hunting for two types of people."

"What's that?" Biggie replied.

"Enemies and informants," Marvin answered.

"If you ain't with us you against us, and if you a rat... we will find you and exterminate you," Gotti said.

"Tell Queen we will get y'all the rest of the money by next week. We still got our crew out here moving them bricks. That gives us time to go rat hunting."

Everyone sat inside the tinted Impala laughing.

After business was over Gotti and Marvin watched as Biggie got out of the car and walked across the street to a Lexus where Zeta was patiently waiting inside.

"Everything good?"

"Yeah, them two niggas is crazy! All they do is sell drugs and go around killing rats," Biggie said.

Zeta laughed out loud and sat back shaking her head.

"What's so damn funny?"

"You," Zeta replied.

"Why am I so funny?"

"Because you said Gotti and Marvin is both crazy. When you do all the same shit. Sell drugs and kill rats."

Biggie laughed as Zeta started the car and drove down the street.

Sitting on the porch right across the street was a guy named Ricky. He was a lower street level dealer working for Gotti and Marvin. Unbeknownst to them all, Ricky was a paid informant for the FBI. Trying his best to get in good with the crew and hopefully gather some vital information to help take them all down.

Later That Evening, Chester, PA

Biggie, Queen, and Zeta watched as their workers removed duffle bags filled with cocaine from the large U-Haul truck. Over 3,000 kilograms of pure cocaine was being carried into a large, private warehouse located in the small city of Chester. Everyone in the organization had been very impressed with Queen's ability to make major moves and run the business while her husband King healed from his injuries.

After all the drugs had been removed from the truck and taken into the warehouse everyone left and went their separate ways.

Philadelphia International Airport

When Vance stepped off the plane, a tinted black Ford Taurus was waiting for him. When he got inside, he was greeted by agents Lucas and Tony. The car pulled off and went through a private gate that was off limits to the public.

"You did a great job down in Miami. We got Paco Vazquez and Rosa Gomez discussing a major drug distribution network operation," Agent Lucas said.

"Paco don't know that we have been aware of him sneaking in and out of the country under anonymous names. After a few more meetings and the delivery of the drugs, we are arresting Rosa and Paco. With that done we will be on the verge of taking down one of the biggest drug cartels in the world, all thanks to you Vance," Agent Tony said, before passing him a black Adidas bag.

"That's $350,000 for a job well done. A small gift from your friends at the FBI," he added.

With a broad smile, Vance sat back in deep thought. Working with the Feds had made him untouchable. They paid him for information and allowed him to murder, kidnap and sell millions of dollars' worth of drugs. He was their biggest puppet. Vance was a man with no conscience, no fear or no loyalty to nothing but power and money.

Chapter 18
Four Seasons Hotel
Washington, DC

Inside a private room on the 3rd floor, King had been waiting patiently. His private nurse and driver were down in the lobby waiting for him. Today King had a very important meeting on his schedule, a meeting that he had to attend once a month, at different locations throughout the East Coast. The month before, the same meeting had taken place in Boston, Massachusetts.

As King sat in a chair, on his lap was a large, black briefcase filled with $2 million in cash. When the door finally opened in walked his infamous cousin, Face, and his right-hand man, Quincy. Face and Quincy shook King's hand and sat down at the small table.

"How are you feeling?" Face asked.

"I'm good. Still rehabbing, but I'll be okay. The meds be helping a lot," King replied.

"I'm hearing a lot of bad things about Philly. You have to continue to stay low key and incognito until things calm down. Your name is all over the place, and the Feds won't stop until they can put you and everyone in your crew away," Face said.

"And what's up with Vance?"

"I found out that he's a major informant who's been working with the Feds for almost 20 years," King answered.

"I should've killed that motherfucker years ago. We heard he was a rat, but we never got any real evidence to verify it. Now it makes sense that he's been out on the streets all this time and never got indicted or arrested," Quincy said.

"Well, I'm married to his daughter! She exposed his rat ass to me," King said.

"Oh, and about your new wife, we heard all about the deal she did with the Mexicans. That's major! You need to keep her close; she is a problem, a good problem," Face said.

"You have to do something about Vance. He can be a major thorn in our side. He's very connected, and the only person that can give you a real challenge for the throne. Do you need me to take care of it?"

"No, no, I got this! My crew and me is good. We can handle Vance's rat ass!" King vented.

Face and Quincy both smiled and nodded their heads in agreement.

King could have easily gotten Face's help to get rid of Vance, but he was determined to eliminate his enemy himself.

"Also, that kid Gotti and his friend Marvin are both good to go," Quincy said, changing the subject.

"He's the real deal. I hear a lot of good things about him. His father is a made member of the Italian Mafia in South Philly. He's a real stand-up guy and loyal also."

King shook his head and said, "Thanks for checking him out for me. You never know who is real these days. I just want to have a real tight crew of loyal, stand-up people that would never snitch because they respect the code of the streets."

"You got me," Face replied. "Just keep Biggie, Queen, Zeta, Gotti and Marvin close, and you will have a long run," he added.

King smiled and pushed the briefcase over to Face. "That's $2 million. Yours and mines," King said.

Face smiled and said, "Keep it up, and one day you'll be as rich as me."

Every month King would give Face an extra million dollars for him to put away in a private offshore account. So that they wouldn't leave a money trail, they would meet up in different cities to collect the cash. Afterward, Face would get back on his private jet and leave the country. So far King had saved up twenty-four million dollars.

"Also make sure you get with my good friend, Luther Dynasty. He's a real estate tycoon. I told him all about you. He's expecting you in his office next Monday at 2 pm," Face said, passing King a small, white card. "Keep investing your money wisely. Remember, nothing in life is promised."

After the meeting had ended everyone left the hotel. While Face and Quincy were headed back to the airport, King headed home to Philly.

Chapter 19
28th & Cumberland
North Philly

Terry and his new goon, Magic, had a whole family tied up in the back room of a small row home. The man, his wife, and three children were seated on the floor. They were all tied up, and their mouths were duct taped. Victor walked into the room with the look of the devil in his eyes. He approached the terrified man and snatched the duct tape off his mouth. The man was noticeably shaken, staring at the loaded 9mm in Victor's hand.

"Where the fuck do King, Biggie or Zeta live?" he asked calmly.

"I swear I don't know where any of them live. I've been out of the game for two years," the man said. "Please don't shoot us!! Please!" the man begged.

"I'm going to ask you again! What do you know about King and anyone in his crew?" Victor asked.

Terry and Magic stood back in silence. With loaded guns in their hands, they were both patiently waiting for Victor to give them the word.

"I know about this stash house they got on Ridge Avenue. They go there once in a while for meetings, counting drug profits and moving cocaine," the man said. At that moment, he would have said anything to save himself and the lives of his family.

After giving Victor the address, he placed the tape back over the man's mouth. Victor looked deep into the man's eyes and said, "I won't shoot you or anyone in your family."

Then he reached around his back and pulled out a 12-inch hunting knife. Victor didn't pay any attention to the tears in their eyes. He was consumed with hate and revenge. Without hesitation Victor slit everyone's throat, killing each one of them.

Moments later, the three men were all walking out of the door, leaving an entire family dead and lying in a large pool of blood.

6th & Arch Street, The Federal Building

Ricky Barnes was a very jealous man. For years, he had been a jealous, manipulative man, secretly plotting to one day take Gotti and Marvin down. It had stemmed from years of being looked over and not respected in the hood. Gotti and Marvin had gotten all the girls, money and fame, and it had been secretly eating at Ricky. No one had ever looked his way. Even he couldn't believe it when Gotti had given him a job to run his drug corner. So, for months Ricky had been secretly gathering info for the FBI. Though they had yet to gather any crucial info on Gotti and Marvin, he did manage to get a few wired conversations on other members of their crew.

As Ricky walked down the hall, he approached a waiting elevator and stepped inside. When he got off on the 4th floor, there were two FBI agents waiting for him. A few people watched as the agents escorted Ricky down the hall and into a back office. One of the men standing around thought he recognized Ricky from somewhere. He knew that Ricky had to be one of two things: a witness or a rat. The guy had some major ties on the streets. In fact, he was well paid just to get information on informants. The man stepped into an empty bathroom and took out his cell phone.

"Yo wassup?" a voice said.

"I might got something for you," he said into the phone.

“Another one? Damn!” the man on the phone said. “Well just find out whatever you can and keep me posted. Find something good, and your money will be in the PO Box,” then the phone went dead.

After leaving the bathroom, the man went searching for answers. He had to find out why the Feds were so hush-hush about the man. He smiled, knowing that in one day he would have all the answers and his money.

Chapter 20
Nassau. The Bahamas

Paco Vazquez and two of his associates stood back and watched as their workers filled a small yacht with pounds of Colombian cocaine. The large shipment of coke was headed to the Florida coast, where a member of Paco's cartel would be waiting. When it arrived in the States, there would be a waiting van that would deliver the drugs to Vance and Rosa in Philadelphia.

Paco had been working with key Bahamian officials to deliver and transport money and drugs in and out of America. His drug cartel was responsible for 60% of the cocaine that entered the US. With a fleet of airplanes, helicopters, and speedboats to distribute drugs to Florida, Colombians had been controlling the cocaine business for decades.

Unbeknownst to Paco and his crew, the FBI, DEA, and Interpol had known everything about them. For years, they had been using undercover informants to gather crucial information, surveillance and secret recordings to bring the entire Cartel down. The government had known all about Paco sneaking in and out of the country. They allowed it just to gather crucial information that would lead them to the head of the Cartel, and bring the entire organization crumbling down. Vance Lewis was their key informant, and if needed the star witness.

For twenty years Vance had been responsible for some of the biggest drug busts on the East Coast. He had a secret FBI file that only a handful of people had full access to. As a paid FBI informant Vance was a valuable individual that the government needed to plant in certain situations. For years Vance had been supplied with government money, drugs and guns to use for deals and to flood the streets. The truth was that the US government was the largest illegal drug organization in the world.

Chapter 21
17th & Market Street
Center City Philadelphia

King stepped off the elevator on the 50th floor of One Liberty Place. He approached an attractive black female secretary sitting behind a huge desk inside the lobby.

"How can I help you, sir?"

"I'm here to meet Mr. Luther Dynasty. I have a 2 o'clock appointment."

"Yes, you are Mr. Smith? He's expecting you," the woman said as she picked up the phone. "Your two o'clock is here," she said. After hanging up the phone, she directed King to the office down the hallway. "It's the last office on the right."

With the help of his cane, King slowly walked down the hall. When he entered the office a large, older, well-dressed Black man was sitting in there waiting for him. Luther Dynasty was black as the night sky, with pearly white teeth that accentuated his big smile. They shook hands, and Luther said, "Glad to meet you, King, you come highly recommended. Plus, I was a big fan of yours when you were at Kansas University. Sorry about the knee injury. You were destined for NBA greatness."

"Thanks, it just wasn't meant to be."

"Do you still play basketball?"

"Not really, I shoot some baskets in my backyard once in a while, but that's about it. But when I'm fully healed from these gunshot wounds I'll be back on the court," King replied.

"So, I hear you're Face's favorite younger cousin, and you need to invest some of your money."

"Yes, but what exactly do you do?" King asked curiously.

"Well I do a lot, but mostly I'm a real estate developer and investor. I also do investment banking, international business ventures and so much more," Luther said proudly.

"Wow, so you're the man for real?"

"I've been told, but trust me it wasn't easy. I earned every penny of my wealth."

"So, what can you do for me?" King asked.

Luther laughed and said, "Help you steer your money and put it in all the right places so it will earn you more. It's about transforming from rich to wealthy. Rockefeller, Goldman, DuPont, Walton and the Koch families are all wealthy. That's my mindset and the mindset I like all my clients to have. The Black man must start thinking like the White man.

Our former slave masters have shown us how to conquer the world of unlimited wealth, but our people are too consumed with helping the white man become wealthier by purchasing their expensive cars, clothes, jewels, and so on. We invest more money into the same people that raped our grandmothers and murdered our fathers than we do in ourselves. We lack knowledge in the world banking system, but we can easily tell you about the latest pairs of Jordan's that's coming out. Our people are blinded by the façade that the white man has created. They want us to believe that they control the entire world, when in fact they don't. They just stole the entire world from under our feet, and every other race on this earth allowed it to happen. But I've studied the blueprint, and I'm willing to teach my brothers the true meaning of wealth. The Forbes list kind of wealth," Luther said.

The more King listened, the more he impressed he was with Luther Dynasty. He was a bold, bright intellectual. Luther Dynasty was a man's, man. He was a Black man that talked and walked with confidence.

"I'm about to invest in a condominium complex on Delaware Avenue. I want you to be a part of it," Luther said.

"How much will that cost me?"

"Three million and I..."

"I will have you a cashier's check tomorrow," King said, cutting him off in mid-sentence.

King was so in awe of Luther that he didn't have to hear all the particulars. If Face believed in Luther Dynasty then why shouldn't he do the same, he thought. For the next two hours they talked, laughed and discussed plans for power and wealth.

Chapter 22
Passyunk Avenue
South Philly

Johnny Marino and Chow-men were letting it be known that a million-dollar bounty had been placed on Vance's head. They were prepared for any problems or war that Vance brought their way. This was about revenge. Together they had over twenty men out looking for Vance or anyone from his crew. The death of their brothers had placed both of their families in chaos. Drama flooded both of their inner circles.

"We have to find and kill that cocksucker!" Johnny vented.

"Don't worry my friend we will. A million dollars will make anyone talk," Chow replied.

Johnny looked at Chow and said, "Let's hope so."

16th & Erie Avenue, North Philly

"What's the emergency Biggie?" Gotti asked.

"Y'all have a rat in your crew!"

"Who is it?" Marvin asked.

"Do you have a worker named Ricky? Ricky Barnes?" Biggie asked both men.

"Yeah, he from around the way. He been with us for a minute. He a rat?" Gotti asked in frustration.

"How did you find out?" Marvin asked.

"Just know that we have a few friends down at the Federal building," Biggie said.

"Find that rat! Find him fast! And when you do call me ASAP!!!"

Gotti and Marvin stood there in total disbelief. They had known Ricky for years, and he had always seemed thorough. That's why they had given him a job working on one of their most lucrative drug corners.

"Let's go find this bitch ass nigga!" Gotti told Marvin.

"Where do you want to start at?"

"His baby mama's house on Lehigh Avenue," Gotti replied.

After putting their jackets on, they rushed out the door and got into a tinted black Impala. When the car pulled off, neither man said a single word, but anger was written on their faces.

24th & Ridge Avenue

Victor, Terry, and Magic sat inside a tinted van watching as all the foot traffic went in and out of a corner row house. "This motherfucker is making a killing out here!" Terry said. With their guns loaded and ready, they watched as a gray BMW pulled up, and a young man carrying a black sports bag calmly stepped out and walked into the house.

"Okay fellas, let's go," Victor said, holding a loaded AK-47. The three men approached the door and quickly kicked it in and rushed inside. The four men inside were caught completely off guard.

"Put your hands up!!" Terry yelled.

All four men were traumatized and did as they were told. Victor walked over to the man with the sports bag and took it from him. The bag was filled with four kilos and $175,000 in cash.

Terry looked at Magic and nodded his head. Then Magic walked behind the terrified man and put his huge arms around his neck. With one strong pull, he broke the man's neck and watched as his lifeless body slumped hard to the floor.

The other three men stood there in complete fear. Victor raised the AK-47 and began chopping each man down.

"My sister dies, so now everyone must pay!" he said before they all rushed out the door and got back in the van.

In less than three minutes, three men were dead, and the other one was still clinging onto his life. He had been shot twice with the AK-47, but death had yet to call his name. Somehow, he had managed to stand up and stagger to the door. People started to approach the house to see what all the commotion was about.

"Somebody call an ambulance!" a woman yelled. "Somebody call 911," she added.

The man fell to the ground, and the woman ran over to console him.

"Hold on baby! Don't die on me!" she said.

"Who did this?" she cried.

"It ... was ... Magic ...," the man said before he finally closed his eyes, joining his three friends on the other side of the light.

Chapter 23
28th & Lehigh
North Philly

"Baby come home now! Something happened to Junior. He's sick!" the woman said into the phone before she hung up.

Gotti and Marvin stood over the woman and her child with 9mm's pointing at their heads.

"Please don't kill me and my son. I did what y'all asked me to do. My son is only eight years old!" she cried out.

"So, you didn't know your boyfriend was a snitch trying to set us up?" Gotti said.

"No, I swear I didn't know! He don't tell me anything," she answered.

The woman wrapped her arms around her son and said, "Stop crying Lil' Ricky, everything is going to be okay."

Gotti and Marvin looked at each other and just shook their heads. It was a tough situation to be in but this was all a part of the life they chose.

"Promise me you won't kill us!" she said. "Please!!"

Before any of them could say another word the front door opened and Ricky ran inside.

"We're in the kitchen," the woman yelled.

As soon as he stepped inside Marvin grabbed him and had his gun at his head.

"You fucking rat!"

They quickly tied Ricky up and placed a bag over his head. His girlfriend and son both watched in pure horror. Marvin then walked Ricky out through the back door while Gotti stayed behind. With duct tape over Ricky's mouth, he wasn't able to talk at all.

"Please don't kill us!" the woman begged.

Gotti looked deep into the woman's teary eyes and said, "It's either you die or I get a life sentence for letting y'all live."

With that said Gotti aimed his 9mm and shot the woman and her son each one once in the head, killing them instantly. As guilt filled his soul, he knew that it was the only thing to do. It was a dirty game, and someone had to do the dirty work.

After pulling off with Ricky in the trunk of the car, they headed to West Philly where Biggie was eagerly waiting.

Chapter 24
Villanova, PA

Inside his lavish six-bedroom home, Luther Dynasty sat at his desk perusing through a pile of business proposals. He had been one of the most sought out businessmen and real estate developers in the country. His wealth was well over a billion dollars, and he was one of the few black men featured on the Forbes list of the 100 wealthiest men.

Face was one of his clients, and that's how he had been introduced to his cousin King. Face wanted King to one day become extremely wealthy, and he knew Dynasty was the right man that could help King make it.

Luther liked his new client a lot. King was an intelligent young man with lots of potential. Luther knew that under his direction King would one day become a man of great wisdom and wealth.

Luther put his folder down and stood up from his desk. He walked over and stared at the different pictures on the wall. For a moment, he just stood there frozen, reminiscing about the troubled life that he had to survive, claw and fight for. Luther Dynasty was a man of mystery.

Wynnewood, PA

King was lying naked on the bed waiting for Queen to get out of the shower. The lights were dimmed, and the smooth sounds of Maxwell flowed out of the speakers. His health was improving day by day, still, he wasn't ready to hit the streets at full stride. Luckily, he had a strong, loyal team that kept everything running smoothly and in order.

Queen stepped out of the shower dripping wet. Seeing her beautiful naked body instantly gave King an erection. He wasn't just in love with his wife; he was in lust, infatuated and in total awe of his queen.

Queen climbed her wet, naked body on top of King and began to slowly massage his dick with her warm mouth. The more King moaned, the more Queen enjoyed pleasing him. She sucked his dick until King couldn't hold back any longer. When he finally came, she caught every single drop of his warm juice.

Chapter 25
West Philly

The gloomy basement felt like a small dungeon. The walls were painted black, with chains and handcuffs hanging all around. A large, steel table was situated in the middle of the room. Biggie, Gotti, and Marvin all stood back in shock watching as Doc had Ricky's naked body chained down on the table.

Doc had a small device inside of Ricky's mouth removing his tongue. He had already removed both of Ricky's eyes. When Doc finished removing his tongue, he walked over to a shelf and grabbed a long, clear, glass tube and a small brown box. No one said a word as they watched Doc walked back over to Ricky's naked body.

Doc stood behind Ricky and inserted the 12-inch clear tube deep inside of his rectum. Instantly Ricky's groans and moans filled the air. Gotti and Marvin had never seen anything so gross. Doc then reached into the box and pulled out a small, white rat. He put the rat inside the tube and then sealed it up. When the rat entered Ricky's anus, Doc pulled the tube out, trapping the rat inside.

"I haven't fed Kiki in two days," Doc said, with a devilish smile.

Seconds later, the rat began eating Ricky's asshole. While Doc stood back admiring his work, Biggie, Gotti, and Marvin were astounded.

"Where did you find this guy from?" Gotti asked Biggie.

"He been around for a while. He is a part of our team," Biggie smiled.

"Can I use him some day?"

"Anytime," Biggie replied.

"Come on fellas, follow me upstairs," Doc said, as he carried a small bowl with Ricky's eyes and tongue inside of it. Inside the kitchen, everyone stood silently nearby and watched as Doc swallowed the eyeballs and ate Ricky's tongue.

"Don't worry; I will make sure Ricky's body is well taken care of," Doc uttered. With that said, Biggie, Gotti and Marvin left the house, leaving Ricky's body in the hands of a psychotic, sociopathic cannibal.

Chapter 26
Northeast Philly

JoAnn Morgan was one of the top criminal defense lawyers in Philly. Because of her spotless record, she had been very sought after. She was also Vance Lewis's secret lover for over five years.

JoAnn had worked clandestinely with the FBI, DEA and other law enforcement agencies. She was one of the few people that had known about Vance being a secret government informant. For years, she had protected his dark secret of being one of the biggest snitches in Philadelphia. She helped Vance, and his friends at the FBI take down some of the most powerful drug kingpins on the East Coast.

Ms. Morgan did it all out of love. She had been madly in love with Vance since meeting him five years earlier. Despite all of his treachery, deceitfulness, disloyalty, and ruthlessness, JoAnn refused to love anyone else. He was her king on the streets and her Daddy in the sheets.

"Get undressed right now!" Vance told her, as he sat down on the edge of the bed. JoAnn did as she was ordered to do. After JoAnn had undressed, Vance told her to get down on her knees and spread her legs apart. Vance then stood behind her and gripped his hand around her neck.

"Bitch I want you to take all of this dick! Do you hear me?"

"Yes, Daddy!"

Vance positioned himself behind her and slid his hard, long dick deep inside of JoAnn's wet, inviting pussy. With a 100 mg Viagra pill roaming through Vance's body, he fucked JoAnn with brutality and pure aggression. Vance fucked her until she almost fainted and slumped hard to the floor.

"Get comfortable. Tonight, you are sleeping on the floor. I want the bed all to myself," he said, as he got up and lay across the large, king sized bed.

"Okay, Daddy!!" JoAnn replied. With his conquest fulfilled, Vance closed his eyes.

West Philly

The secret stash house was located a few blocks away from the 30th Street Amtrak Train Station. It was near the Drexel University campus. On the top floor of the small, two story home, King, Queen, Zeta, Biggie, Gotti, and Marvin sat around discussing the recent events going on all over Philly. In the past two weeks, over seven men had been murdered or kidnapped from both rival gangs. The FBI, DEA and even Homeland Security were all over Philly and the tri-state area hoping to find answers. DA Candice Shaw also had her secret task force on the streets working with informants.

"We have to shut everything down for a while," King said.

"But why?" Biggie replied.

"Because we can't keep losing good men and money," King answered.

"We have to be smarter than our enemies. They are out searching for us and burning down and robbing all our drug houses in the process," he added.

"So, then what are we going to do?" Gotti asked.

"It's time to stop playing checkers with these guys and start playing chess," Queen replied.

"She's right," King said. "We will continue to sell drugs, but only weight. A half kilo and up and only to our most loyal customers. That will stop all the robberies and murders. Also in the bag on the table are six new untraceable cell phones that I had Roscoe activate for us. We can't afford to slip up out here. Queen and Biggie will continue to run the day-to-day. Zeta will control the wholesale distribution and Gotti, and Marvin will run the streets. I have a meeting in a few hours with my new business partner and financial advisor. We will meet back here in a few days," King said, as everyone stood up from their seats and said their goodbyes.

Moments later, they were all inside their cars headed in different directions.

Northeast Philly

"We will be indicting and arresting Paco Vazquez and Rosa Gomez in the next few weeks." Agent Tony told Vance.

"But why so soon? And why Rosa?"

Agent Lucas walked up to Vance and said, "I know Rosa is your good friend, but we don't pay you, protect you and help you stay out here on the streets to make friends. We pay you to help us bring down drug kingpins. We will also be indicting your Russian mafia associate Victor Gavrikov. We should have already arrested him and his crazy sister."

"That will ruin my entire organization if y'all arrest my connections and my enforcer. How will I survive out here? How will I compete?" Vance said upsettingly.

"We will find you more. There's a new drug dealer showing up every day. But right now, we have to take Rosa and Paco down. She is too powerful on the East Coast, and Paco is the major fish we have been trying to take down for many years. Now that we have him on wire tape and surveillance, incriminating himself and his entire organization, it is time to bring them all down. Hopefully one of them will flip," Agent Tony said.

"Plus, there are a few powerful politicians involved with this case. Elections are coming up soon; they need to show the public that they are tough on crime, drug dealers, and corruption." Agent Lucas added.

Vance sat back in silence, letting everything they said sink in. The one thing he feared was being exposed as a snitch. For years, the Feds had protected his darkest secret of being a paid government informant. Then he stood up and said, "Fuck it! They need to go! But Rosa has to die, she knows too much and will eventually figure it all out."

Agent Lucas walked over to Vance and said, "That won't be a problem. We've done it before, and we can do it again."

Chapter 27
One Week Later
Ridge Avenue

Biggie pulled up and parked his new Lexus Coupe in the parking lot at the BP Gas station. A moment later Gotti and Marvin pulled up behind him in the tinted Impala. Standing nearby was an attractive, tall, brown skinned woman. She was dressed in a pair of blue jeans, a black leather jacket and a pair of UGG boots. Shifting her weight from one foot to the other, it was apparent that she was very nervous. After Biggie beeped the horn, she quickly approached his car and got inside.

"Hi, I'm Dimplez," she said.

"What's up Dimplez?" Biggie said with a smile. Her beauty was captivating. "So, what's it you got for me?"

After a long sigh, Dimplez said, "your friend told me who shot him before he died in my arms."

Biggie's eyes lit up with excitement. "He told you? What did he say? Who did it?"

"He said it was a guy named Magic that shot and killed your friends inside that house," Dimplez replied.

"Magic!" Biggie said, shaking his head.

"Yes, that's what he told me." Biggie reached under his seat and took out a small brown bag. Then he passed it to Dimplez and said, "Thanks a lot, pretty. This is yours. I really appreciate you reaching out to me. Does anyone else know this?"

"No, I didn't tell anybody but you. I'm afraid to say anything. You never know who you're talking to. All I know is that they were your friends that got murdered. I don't need no trouble coming my way. I have two children to take care of," Dimplez said seriously.

"Two kids and a man?" Biggie asked curiously.

"No, just two kids and me." Dimplez smiled.

"That's good to know. Because you're very pretty. You should be a model somewhere."

"I used to model, but that's another story," Dimplez said.

"Well maybe you can tell me all about it one day," Biggie replied.

"Maybe so. You got my number," Dimplez said as she started blushing.

"I'm not too short for you, am I?" Biggie asked.

Dimplez looked at Biggie and said, "Not at all, you're a little cutie, and I heard a lot of good things about you short guys."

"Oh really?" Biggie replied.

"That's just what I heard. Don't know if it's true or not," Dimplez flirted.

"I'll call you," Biggie said before Dimplez got out of the car and walked away.

After Dimplez had vanished from sight, Biggie pulled off with Gotti and Marvin close behind.

Back inside her small two-room apartment, Dimplez walked into her children's bedroom to check on them. Her twin 6-year-old girls were still sound asleep. She then walked into her bedroom and sat down on the bed. Dimplez took out the brown bag and looked inside. Her eyes lit up after seeing all the twenty dollar bills stacked inside. She sat back and counted it. When she finished, it was $5,000 in cash. Dimplez couldn't believe her fortune. Before meeting Biggie, she only had $12.37 cents to her name. Tears rolled down her cheeks as she sat there bemused.

Diana "Dimplez" Mathis was once a top upcoming model in Philadelphia. She had done spreads in national magazines as well as a few TV commercials. Then one day her beautiful world suddenly came crashing down when two masked men broke into her home and killed her husband. One of the men had tied her and the twins up in a back room, while the other man shot her husband in the head. That tragedy left Dimplez traumatized.

For a while, she suffered from PTSD and other social issues. Her late husband, Nino, was her and the kids' life. Since his tragic death Dimplez was a lost woman, in search of a place of happiness ... anything that would get her out of a world of misery and poverty.

Chapter 28
Wynnewood, PA

King relaxed on the sofa and listened as Queen discussed business with the new connects. After she ended the call, Queen walked over and sat down beside him.

"They just received their money, and they are very pleased," she said with a smile.

"You did a good job, and they seem to really like you," King said as he laid his head in Queen's lap.

"Just like most men. They like and yearn for what they can't have. Any man that lusts after me is a potential mark," Queen said as she began running her fingers through King's hair. "We have a new shipment coming in a few days. Me, Zeta and Biggie will make sure everything is taken care of."

"I know y'all will, but I should be back soon. I'm feeling a lot better." King said.

"Just take your time babe, no need to rush. Your team got you covered," Queen said as she kissed King on the lips.

Germantown

Vance stood up in a crowded room surrounded by all his crew. "I'm the reason grown men sleep with their guns and hide their money!" Everyone in the room started to cheer.

"We run this city! We are going to crush anyone that stands in our way! The city is ours!" he shouted.

Terry, Rosa, Victor, and Magic all stood there with smiling faces. They all believed in Vance. He was their boss and mentor, a man they all admired. Because of Vance they were all rich and feared on the streets. Vance raised his right arm, and all the noise instantly ceased.

He looked around the quiet room and said, "King is dead in Philly! Every drug or stash house he had is now closed down! He is a scared little boy. And I won't stop until he is a dead man!!"

Once again, everyone started to cheer. The truth was that King was far from dead, and Vance knew it. Still, he would do whatever it took to convince his crew otherwise.

One Hour Later

Queen looked over and watched as King peacefully slept. He meant the world to her, and there was nothing she wouldn't do for him. She was deeply in love with her husband, and everyone knew it. But deep down inside she knew that as long as her father, Vance, was still alive, they were both in danger.

Vance was a powerful man throughout all of Philly. He had just as many friends and connections as King. Lawyers, hit men and crooked cops were on both of their payrolls. Queen knew that for them to both live the life they wanted, Vance and his crew had to be exterminated. With tears rolling from her eyes Queen put her arms around King and cuddled up next to him.

While Vance stood back smoking a blunt, one of his loyal street lieutenants walked over to him. "Hey boss man," he said.

"Hey, Krack what's up with you?" Vance replied.

"Nothing much just wanted to thank you for giving me another chance."

Vance stared into the short, brown skinned man's eyes and said, "Krack you are one of my top men. I need you out here, but you need to stay far away from the bottle. You can't keep getting drunk on the job. You run my West Philly distribution, I need you on point at all times, or I will have to replace you with someone else. Don't let being drunk be your downfall," Vance said with all seriousness.

Krack stood there shaking his head in agreement.

"Just keep doing your job and stay away from the bottle. You can call me, Terry, or Victor at any time. But right now, I need you to continue working with John Carter and all the others to help me lock West Philly down."

"I'm on it boss man. I like working with the cop," Krack said as they both started to laugh.

"Yeah, he's a dirty motherfucker ain't he?"

"Yes, he is, but I'm glad he's on our team," Krack laughed.

Chapter 29
23rd & Diamond
North Philly

Biggie, Gotti, and Marvin watched the house from across the street. Inside a stolen minivan, they patiently waited for Magic to return home. After waiting an hour, Biggie decided that it was time to make a move. He knew that Magic lived there with his mother and younger brother. With black ski masks covering their faces, the three of them got out of the van and ran across the street. With a powerful kick, Marvin smashed in the front door, and they all rushed inside.

Sitting on the couch watching TV was Magic's mother and brother. They were both frightened beyond words. Without hesitation Gotti aimed his 9mm at the mom and shot her once in the head, killing her where she sat. The attached silencer had muffled the sound. Biggie and Marvin rushed over and grabbed Simon and dragged his body out the door.

"He too heavy," Marvin said.

"Well fuck it then!" Biggie said as he pointed his gun at the boy's head and squeezed the trigger. POW!!! The .40 caliber shot off a large piece of Simon's brain. Blood, bones and brain matter splattered on the curb.

They all rushed back over to the stolen van and sped off down the dark, empty street. "I'm not playing with these motherfuckers no more!" Biggie said.

Twenty minutes later, they all stood back and watched as the minivan was torched and engulfed in flames, making sure there was no evidence left behind. They then walked a block away from the burning van and got back into their waiting cars. Biggie pulled out of the parking spot and drove down the street. Gotti and Marvin drove off in the opposite direction. Biggie decided to drive home, but Gotti and Marvin weren't finished with a night that was going to be filled with murder.

When Biggie walked into his home, he showered and got into bed. Then he reached for his cell phone and called a number.

"Hello?" a beautiful voice answered.

"Hey, Dimplez. I had you on my mind all night!" he said with a smile.

Chapter 30
Early the Next Morning

Magic stood behind the yellow police tape in tears. Standing beside him were Victor and Terry. He was in total shock after learning that his mother and brother had both been savagely murdered. Even though no one saw a thing, Magic had known in his heart who the responsible people were. He stood there fuming with anger.

"King and Biggie are going to die for this!!" he mumbled.

As tears continued to fall down his face, he turned and walked back over to the car. Victor and Terry followed him, but neither one had said a word. After they were all back inside the car, Victor slowly pulled away from the curb and drove away. Each one of them had the same mission and purpose; to find and kill King, Biggie, and Zeta.

Mercy Medical Center, Baltimore, MD

After a long, six-hour delivery Sofie had finally given birth to a seven pound, three-ounce baby boy. She named her son Solomon, after the great King of Israel and son of David. After the nurse placed Solomon in her arms, Sofie tearfully stared into her son's beautiful hazel eyes. She kissed him on his soft cheeks and smiled with joy. The only person who had known about her child was her sister Robin, or at least that's what Sofie thought.

Unbeknownst to Sofie and Robin, they had been secretly watched for months. Queen hired a private investigator to find Sofie. When he found out where she was, he was to report everything back to Queen.

As Sofie lay in bed breastfeeding her newborn baby boy, she couldn't help but think about Queen and King. Since shooting King and almost taking his life, Sofie had feared for her own life. She was one of the few people that knew about Queen's jealousy and wrath. Behind Queen's beauty and brains, she was a cold-blooded femme fatale.

Chapter 31
Center City

King sat across the desk from his new business partner, Luther Dynasty.

"The new deal has gone through; I just need you to sign these papers and everything is a go. Also, I added your wife and two friends to the new deal like you requested. They will each receive significant shareholder's profits," Luther said as he passed King a few papers and a black pen.

"Thanks, Luther, I really appreciate you for this."

"No problem, I think it's admirable what you are doing for your close friends. It tells me a lot about your character. You care and love the people you got around you. We are going to make millions together; this is only the beginning." Luther smiled.

After signing all the papers both men stood up and shook hands.

"You're the man, Luther. Now I see why my cousin Face trusts you with his money."

As King turned and walked towards the door, Luther said, "Just stay focused out on those streets. Don't get caught up in the hype. Stay invisible while you conquer."
King nodded his head and smiled before he walked out of the office.

~~~

JoAnn Morgan sat on the toilet staring at the positive pregnancy test. For weeks, she suspected that she was pregnant. Feeling tired, throwing up her food and feeling moody were a few symptoms she had been dealing with. She had desperately wanted a child with Vance, but she knew that Vance didn't. He told her many times that "I'm not
~~~

interested in any more kids." As she sat there, confusion consumed her mind and soul.

JoAnn walked out of the bathroom and into the living room, then sat down at the computer and Googled nearby abortion centers. It would be her fourth abortion in two years. She didn't want to go to the same abortion clinic because she would be embarrassed having to return to the same location for a fourth time. JoAnn hated the fact that she couldn't have a child with the man she loved. Each time she terminated a pregnancy, it ate at her soul. A child is all that she ever wanted, but somehow life had prevented JoAnn from becoming a mother.

12:18 A.M., 52nd & Chestnut St, West Philly

Gotti and his right-hand man, Marvin, were out driving around looking for anyone that was associated with Vance's drug organization. They were both loyal soldiers to King's crew. Not only were they cold-blooded killers but they were also two of the top drug dealers in the city. King supplied them with drugs to move and guns to kill.

On the corner of 52nd and Chestnut, they spotted a known member of Vance's crew. It was Krack, a top street lieutenant in Vance's organization. Krack was noticeably drunk, staggering over to his parked BMW.

"Got one!" Gotti said, as they quickly pulled over and jumped out of the car with guns aiming at Krack's head. In less than a minute Krack was in the darkness of the Impala's trunk, kicking and begging for his life.

Twenty minutes later, Marvin pulled up and parked behind the Target on City Line Avenue. They got out of the car and popped open the trunk.

"Please don't kill me!" Krack said, looking at the two guns pointed at his head.

"Do you know who we are?" Gotti asked.

"The stick-up boys?" Krack replied.

Gotti looked deep into Krack's eyes and said, "No, we are the Grim Reapers if you don't tell us what we need to know!"

Before Krack could say a word his cell phone started to ring. Marvin reached into his jacket pocket and took out his cell phone.

"Dirty cop," Marvin said.

"Who is this?" he asked.

"It's John Carter; he is a cop that we work with from the 18th District!" Krack replied in fear.

Gotti and Marvin both smiled. "Is that right?" Gotti said.

"Please man, don't kill me!!" Krack said as Marvin pulled him out of the trunk. As he lay on the ground drunk and confused Gotti and Marvin didn't hesitate to unload their entire clips into Krack's head and body.

Moments later, Marvin was driving down Belmont Avenue, Gotti was riding shotgun and going through all the messages on Krack's cell phone.

"Jackpot!" Gotti said.

Two Days Later, Ridge Avenue

"Oh god! Yes, Daddy! Yes!" Dimplez screamed out in ecstasy. Biggie had Dimplez's long legs spread wide apart, as he fucked her with every muscle in his short, stocky body. Dimplez lay on her back breathing hard and heavy, as continuous orgasms swept through her trembling body. Biggie's long, fat dick was a total surprise. Even though he was a short man, he was a very dominant lover.

As he continued to fuck Dimplez all over the bed, tears of joy ran from her eyes. Her loud moans filled the bedroom. "Fuck your pussy Daddy! Beat your pussy up!" Biggie turned Dimplez on her stomach and slid his thick dick deep inside of her pink, wet pussy.

While he fucked her from behind Biggie pulled her hair back and bit the back of Dimplez's neck. It drove her wild and crazy as her tall, slim body began to tremble beneath him.

"This is my pussy from now on!" he yelled.

"Yes Daddy, this is all yours!" Dimplez answered. Dimplez laid there lost for words. She was caught in a world of pure pleasure and dominance. She had never been fucked so well in all her life.

After Biggie finished fucking her from behind, he lay back with his hands behind his head and watched as Dimplez sucked his thick, 8-inch dick. After exploding inside her mouth, he laid beside her. After a brief break, he climbed back on top of her and had Dimplez screaming, moaning and calling for God again.

While Dimplez's two daughters were in school, they fucked like there was no tomorrow. At 2:30 Biggie left so that she could get her daughters from the nearby school at 3 pm. Before he drove off, Biggie said, "I will call you later tonight and see you in the morning."

"Okay, Daddy. I can't wait," Dimplez said, smiling.

Chapter 32
The 18th Police District
West Philly

Officer John Carter walked out of the Police Station and got into his car that was parked out front. John Carter was a man disliked by many of his peers. All throughout the Police Force, he had been known as a crooked cop. With over ten years on the force, he had been investigated by the Internal Affairs Division a dozen times. Each time he managed to somehow escape charges that would cost him his job. Rumors around the station were that John was a paid member of the Vance Lewis drug organization. No one had proof of whether it was true or not. John checked a text message on his cell phone before pulling off down the street.

"On my way now," he texted back.

Ten minutes later, John pulled up and parked his car in front of a house on 58th & Hazel Street. After getting out of his car he walked up the porch steps and strolled into the house.

"Krack! Krack where youse at?" he shouted out.

"I'm upstairs," a voice said.

John Carter walked up the stairs and headed to the back room. Suddenly Gotti and Marvin rushed out of a room behind him. Each were holding a loaded 9mm pistol.

"What the..."

"Shut the fuck up and walk into the room," Gotti said, pointing his gun at John's back.

John Carter raised his arms and did as he was told. When he stepped into the room, his eyes lit up. Standing there were King, Biggie, and Zeta.

"Sit down officer," King said.

John sat in the chair that was centered in the middle of the room. Marvin reached inside his jacket and removed his cell phone and gun.

"You won't be needing these," he said.

"Where's Krack?" he asked.

King walked up to John and said, "I think you know the answer to that already."

John looked down and just shook his head. "I have a family, two kids and a wife."

"Then just tell me what I need to know, and maybe you will get to see them again one day," King replied.

Chapter 33
Two Days Later
Cottman Avenue, Northeast Philly

"Where the fuck is Krack!" Vance shouted out to a small group of his most loyal men.

"I been calling and texting his phone all morning," Terry said.

Vance stood there shaking his head. He had given Krack so many opportunities and chances. Magic, Victor, and a few others all stood around in silence.

"Terry, after this meeting I need you to go find that nigga and bring him to me," Vance said.

"Alright, boss," Terry replied.

"And what's going on with King, any new info?"

"Nothing so far. All of his drug houses are closed down. He has also shut down his business. We can't find anything on him or anyone in his crew," Victor answered. Vance shook his head and said, "Something is going on with him. He's up to something. Make sure John Carter knows this so he can find out what's going on," Vance said.

"John has been MIA also. He hasn't been answering his cell phone, and no one has seen or talked to him," Victor answered.

Vance stood there in disbelief. He could tell that something was wrong. This wasn't like Krack or John. They had never disappeared without letting someone know. Vance was dealing with a lot of shit. The Feds, his beef with King and now two top members of his crew had suddenly vanished.

"We have to be smart out on the streets. Something don't feel right, and I know that bitch ass nigga King and my traitor daughter Queen are up to no good."

As Vance was talking Terry's cell phone started ringing. "Hello?" he answered. "What! Are you serious?" Then he ended the call.

"Who was that?" Vance asked, after seeing the disturbing look on Terry's face.

"I found Krack," Terry said.

"Where is that nigga?"

Terry looked into Vance's eyes, and after a long sigh he said, "He's in the morgue, been in there for three days."

North Philly

Computer geek and professional hacker Roscoe sat at his desk patiently waiting for Gotti and Marvin to arrive. Thirty minutes later they pulled up and parked right outside of his home. Roscoe let them inside, and they all walked down to the basement. Two large monitors and a row of Apple computers were situated along a table. Piles of computer books and other paperwork were stacked against a wall. Roscoe was one of the top computer hackers on the East Coast. He had the skills to breach defenses and exploit weaknesses in any computer system or network.

"Wassup fellas? What's so important?" Roscoe asked. Marvin passed Roscoe John Carter's cell phone and said, "I need you to get all the information off this phone. We need to put numbers with addresses or people. We need to know about every contact on this phone."

Roscoe analyzed the cell phone thoroughly and responded, "No problem, just give me a little time and I will have everything y'all need. Where he pays his bills, credit card accounts, emails, addresses, private and personal links and anything else."

"That's good. We will see you soon," Gotti said, before passing Roscoe five one hundred dollar bills. Moments later,

Gotti and Marvin were back inside the car calling King on his cell phone.

"He has the phone; everything will be taken care of soon."

"Fine. I'm gonna need that info as soon as possible," King said before ending the call.

Allenwood Federal Prison

After pleading out to a 40-year sentence for drug possession and distribution, Tito Vazquez had become numb to everything. He didn't trust anyone but his cousin Rosa. After learning some crucial information about his case, he sat at his small desk and started to write Rosa a letter. He needed her to know about everything he recently learned. There was more to his federal drug case than he had known. Tito was now determined to help expose the secrets of the US Government, how they operated and how they used the closest people to you to make them cooperate and bring you down.

Chapter 34
A Few Days Later

Johnny Marino and Chow-men added another 500 grand on top of the million-dollar bounty that was already on Vance's head. In less than an hour, the word had spread all throughout the Philly underworld. $1.5 million would make men do things that they wouldn't normally do. The streets were now hungry for blood. Johnny and Chow knew that it was just a matter of time before someone came with information about Vance or brought them his head.

Baltimore, MD

Sofie and baby Solomon were inside the comfort of her bedroom. As Sofie laid in bed breastfeeding her son she couldn't help but reminisce about her true love, Queen. Queen had always been the real love of her life, but circumstances had broken them apart and created their current distance.

As Sofie watched her son nurse from her breast tears began to fall from her eyes. She felt confused, lost and very lonely. The only family she had was her half-sister, who was hardly ever home. She was too busy running the streets, stripping at clubs and chasing after the wrong men. She didn't approve or want anything to do with that life. She had a baby now, and Sofie was determined to raise herself a king.

~~~

JoAnn Morgan walked out of the Women's Health Center in tears. Once again, she had terminated another pregnancy. She was crushed, and all she could do was cry in sorrow. After getting back into her car, JoAnn headed back to her empty Northeast home. She took a long, warm shower
~~~

and slipped on one of Vance's XXL T-shirts to feel his closeness.

With the TV remote in hand, she searched through the TV menu until she found a show she was pleased with. The show was called Scandal, a story about a beautiful black educated woman, caught up in a secret relationship with the wrong man. The story of my life she thought. An hour later, JoAnn was lying across the bed crying herself to sleep.

Chapter 35
North Philly

Vance was incensed beyond all words. Another one of his top street lieutenants had been savagely murdered, and no one had seen or heard a thing. Inside a secret stash house near 19th and Jefferson Vance looked around the room at all of his top men. Victor, Terry, and Magic each sat in silence. They could all plainly see that Vance was beginning to stress over the war with King, Biggie and now his oldest daughter, Queen.

He hated Queen for being disloyal and he wouldn't rest until he made her severely pay for crossing him. Choosing her father's enemy over him constantly weighed heavy on his mind and heart.

Suddenly Vance had an epiphany. He stood up and said, "Her bank! Her bank!"

"What bank boss?" Victor asked.

"Queen's bank. She goes there every Monday to deposit money. It's always been her routine; she never misses going to the bank early Monday mornings!!" Vance said with excitement. "Queen uses Bank of America. She mostly uses the one on City Avenue, near the Boston Market," he added. Everyone stood around with smiles on their faces. "If we can get to Queen we can end this goddamn war with King. She will break and tell us everything," Vance said.

"We on it boss!" Terry replied. "I will put a bullet right through her head," he added.

Vance walked up to Terry and said, "I don't want her dead, I want her tortured and humiliated for being disloyal. I want her to lose all that beauty. All her love for that nigga

King will be tested. She has always had it good. She don't know pain like the pain that I'm going to inflict on her ass!" Everyone nodded their heads in agreement.

After a brief conversation, the plan was now to kidnap Queen.

Chapter 36
Camden, NJ

Rosa Gomez couldn't believe the letter that she had just received from her cousin Tito. Tito was currently serving a 40-year federal sentence at Allenwood prison in upstate Pennsylvania. The letter said:

To my dear cousin, I've had a lot of time to think about how I ended up in this place. I went from the biggest in the game to now serving a 40-year sentence because of an informant. For months, the government had refused to give my lawyers the proper paperwork, so I could see who was involved with helping to bring me down. Because I had plead out, my team was limited to certain court documents and my secret FBI file.

But this past week I had finally gotten two letters from the FBI about my conspiracy and drug conviction. The letter was a bunch of bullshit, stuff about my case that I had already known. But there are a few names that were blackened out to hide the informant's identity. I don't want to jump to any conclusions but I want you to pay very close attention to your friend Vance. My gut feeling is that he had something to do with my arrest.

I've had my people check out everyone that I had a personal and business relationship with and Vance is the only person that was close enough to bring me down. My lawyers can't find nothing on this guy.

Plus, I learned that the two previous connects he had are also behind bars, each serving life sentences. Still, not one person has ever mentioned his name on their case. But something don't feel right. Rosa just watch yourself and be careful around Vance and his crew. Maybe I'm wrong about this and Vance is the stand-up guy you said he was when you introduced us, but you rather be safe than sorry.

After reading the letter, Rosa sat back in deep thought. Her mind was clouded with lots of thoughts. All she could do was sit back and shake her head.

West Philly

John Carter had never felt more humiliated in all his life. For three days, he had been a kidnapped victim, locked away in Doc's basement of terror and torture. King had John dropped off at Doc's to see if he could get any answers from the dirty cop. So far, John had refused to say a word. He knew that death was inevitable and he would most likely never see his wife and children again.

Doc was told to keep John alive. Doc had John's naked body chained to a long, wooden table. He had been severely beaten and burned. Both of John's eyes and lips were swollen from being constantly punched and slapped in his face. To keep John from starving to death, Doc fed him human flesh from a previous victim.

"Did he say anything yet?" King asked Doc over the phone.

"Not yet, he's one tough cookie to crack. You should just let me end his misery," Doc replied.

"No, not yet. He is going to come in handy one day."

"Ok King, it is your call," Doc said before they ended the call.

Doc walked over to John and stared deeply into his green eyes. Then he reached down and grabbed his dick and said, "One day, this will be my lunch along with those beautiful eyes." Then with a sadistic laugh, Doc turned and walked out of the basement, leaving John in complete darkness.

The Philadelphia police had an all-out search in place to find Officer John Carter. His disappearance had been featured on all the local news stations. There was also a $100,000 reward for any information that would lead to him being found alive. Law enforcement had known that foul play was involved because John Carter would never leave his wife and children alone without first telling them his whereabouts.

District Attorney Candice Shaw was really dealing with a ton of heat from her superiors. In the past few weeks, two officers had been murdered, and one had suddenly disappeared. With all the violence, drugs and murder on the mean streets of Philly, it was beginning to take a toll on her. Her bosses were in the process of starting an investigation into her office, and if there were any more problems, Candice Shaw would likely face administrative leave and possibly other disciplinary actions.

Chapter 37
Two Days Later
Tokyo, Japan

Luther Dynasty was a man of great power, influence, and wealth. Inside a large conference room at the Mitsui Garden Hotel, Luther was surrounded by a large group of Japanese and European investors. He was negotiating a new deal to build two new sports complexes and shopping malls in Tokyo and London.

In the meeting, King sat quietly in a chair next to Luther. Luther had invited his young protégé to the three-day trip and business meeting in Japan. He wanted to show King the other side of the game, the game that billionaires play on a daily basis. After the meeting had adjourned, they went to the lobby and talked over drinks.

"So, what do you think?" Luther asked.

"You ain't no joke! I was very impressed with how you got all those men to believe in your vision and invest in the project."

Luther smiled and nodded his head.

"You can be big if you follow my lead, King. You have the smarts and the attitude to one day become a successful businessman."

"You really believe so? Just like my cousin Face?" King asked.

"Yes, just like Face. You both remind me a lot of each other."

King smiled and said, "Why didn't you invite Face, he would have definitely invested in a project of this magnitude?"

Luther laughed and said, "I didn't have to invite Face."

"Why not?"

"Because Face is one of my silent investors. He is behind me as the voice to go around the world getting major deals done. Face knew that I was bringing you to Japan, he wants you to start seeing the bigger picture."

"I do, I started to see that there is a much bigger world outside of Philly."

Luther placed his hand on King's shoulder and said, "Right. A world with no limits and endless opportunities."

When King got back into his lavish hotel room, he quickly called Queen on his cell phone. They had talked for almost an hour before he said, "I will be home in two days."

"Okay baby, take your time. You needed a vacation and some time away from all the drama. I love you."

"I love you more. See you soon," he told her.

Hilton Hotel, City Avenue

Terry sat inside of his tinted Range Rover and watched as the two white men walked out of the front entrance and got into their car. For years, he had been seeing these same two men having private meetings with Vance. He had always been suspicious of who they were.

Vance told Terry that the two men were his business partners, but something about them just wasn't right. It was their demeanors that made Terry feel very uncomfortable. Terry always felt that Vance was hiding something from him and that the two white men were more than just business partners. For instance, Vance had never introduced him to them, and most of the meetings they had were usually in hotels throughout the city. Rosa didn't trust them at all, but no one dared question Vance's decisions or authority. He had made them all rich, and neither of them had ever been arrested.

When Vance got back into the Range, he said, "Any word on John yet?"

"Nothing so far," Terry said as he pulled off.

"I'm telling you Terry something ain't right!"

"Don't worry; we will hear something soon."

"Is everything ready for tomorrow morning?" Vance asked as he lit a Cuban cigar.

"Yes, we got everything in order. Me, Rosa and Magic will take care of everything."

"What about Victor?"

"He said he needed some personal time away. I think his sister's death is fucking with him more than he says." Vance nodded his head, blowing a thick cloud of gray smoke into the air.

"Wassup with these two guys you be doing business with?" Terry said, changing the subject.

"Ain't nothing up. They helping me get some things straight. Why do you ask?" Vance said curiously.

After stopping at a red-light Terry said, "I just don't trust them! They act like cops! I'm telling you, Vance; I think they might be the Feds."

Vance laughed and said, "You think too much! They are just my business partners."

"I hope so because I can't stand the Feds or the snitches that work for them."

Vance smiled and said, "Me either. I wish they all die." With that said, Terry smiled and they drove away.

Chapter 38

While King was away on his three-day business trip Queen, Zeta and Biggie ran the drug business. After closing all the drug houses, King had all his street workers use their burner phones to conduct sales. By making this move, he prevented his men from getting kidnapped or murdered by the Vance organization.

At the same time, Gotti and Marvin were still out searching for anyone associated with the enemy. So far, they had murdered or kidnapped several top members of Vance's crew. They were a major asset for King's drug organization. They were the enforcers that King needed to do all the dirty work.

After the tragic death of his younger sister, Victor hadn't been the same. He had become more distant from everyone. Natasha's death had placed him in a dark place. All he could think about was killing all the people involved with her murder. Nightmares would constantly wake him from his sleep. Inside his home, Victor laid across his large king sized bed clutching a loaded .45 caliber pistol. A boiling rage built up in the deepest part of his dark soul.

Looking at a photo of his sister he said, "I promise you, Natasha, they will all pay for taking you away from me! Each and every single one of them will feel my wrath."

Ridge Avenue

Dimplez was on all fours on the floor of her bedroom. Biggie was crouched behind her, gripping her hips, fucking her hard and intense. Her twin daughters were asleep in the next room, unable to hear the loud moans that escaped their mother's mouth. Biggie stroked Dimplez's pussy like a man possessed.

He had always had a short man's complex, so whenever he had sex with a much taller woman, he made sure he did a job well done. With an eight-inch dick, Biggie took Dimplez to new sexual heights. His stroke game was unlike anyone she had ever experienced. Throughout the night, Biggie made Dimplez cum continuously. As the orgasms swept throughout her drained body, Biggie fucked her like he had something to prove.

Chapter 39
Cedarbrook Cemetery

Magic stood a few feet away from the two tombstones with his mother and brother's names engraved on them. He still couldn't believe they were both gone, or that they had been so savagely killed. He made a personal promise to himself to one day avenge their deaths and kill King and Biggie.

Under the darkness of the sky, tears fell down Magic's face. Before tonight he hadn't cried in over ten years. But the pain that roamed inside of him wouldn't prevent his falling tears. Ten minutes later, Magic walked out of the cemetery and got back inside his car. With the music playing all Magic could do was cry and focus on murder and revenge.

Gotti and his best friend Marvin were once again driving around on an all-out manhunt. They were determined to search, find and kill anyone that was associated with Vance's drug crew. After leaving the Vanity Grand strip club, they decided to drive to the Onyx strip club. They knew that most drug dealers went to the strip club to show off, and spend money on bottles service and naked women. With loaded weapons on the floor of the car, they headed to the Onyx with bad intentions.

Doc had pulled up a chair and sat in front of John's beaten naked body. For almost an hour he just sat there and stared at him. Doc was obsessed with his newest victim and he couldn't wait to taste his flesh.

John Carter didn't know what to think of his capture. He did know one thing, and that was that the strange white man seated in front of him was a psychopathic maniac. Still, John refused to be broken. He knew that once he had given him the info they wanted he would be killed. John knew that he was prolonging the inevitable. Death was the only outcome.

Chapter 40
Early the Next Morning
Ridge Avenue

Dimplez leaned down and kissed Biggie before he walked over to the front door. Once again, they had been locked into a night of wild sex.

"I left the money for you to move out of here on the dresser," Biggie said.

"Thanks, Daddy, I will start looking for a new place for me and the girls as soon as possible. I really appreciate you, Daddy."

"Just get up out of here, this neighborhood ain't safe," Biggie said as he placed his loaded .40 caliber under his shirt.

Dimplez stood in the doorway and watched as Biggie walked to his car and got inside. Moments later, he pulled off.

When Dimplez returned to her bedroom, she took the money from the dresser and sat down on the bed. Biggie had given her $5,000 to move out of her apartment and find someplace new for herself and her twin daughters. The neighborhood where Dimplez lived was one of the most violent and dilapidated in the entire city.

Right across the street from Dimplez's apartment a female had been looking out of the window. She had seen Biggie coming and going for the last few weeks. Her name was Lakisha Jones, a short, dark skinned woman with an average face and thick body. Lakisha sat back contemplating on what she should do.

Her ex-boyfriend, Magic, worked with the Vance Lewis drug crew. A part of her wanted to stay out of it, but the other side was still loyal to Magic. She knew who Biggie was and that most likely he was involved in the double homicide of Magic's mom and little brother. A few times she and Biggie had locked eyes. She noticed that he always checked his surroundings after he parked his car and got out.

After taking a long, deep breath, Lakisha grabbed her cell phone and started texting. A moment later a text came back to her phone saying: "Thanks, love; I will check it out." Then Lakisha laid in bed with her newborn baby and went back to sleep.

Chapter 41
Monday Morning
Downtown Philly

JoAnn Morgan sat back and listened as the FBI agent explained the newest direction for Vance Lewis. She had been summoned to be a part of this secret meeting by the assistant FBI director himself.

"This year the Vance Lewis subject will be involved in a few major cases. Over the past year, he was able to infiltrate two of the top drug cartels in the world. With Vance's help, we have taken down the Tito "Mad Man" Vazquez organization. Now we are on the verge of doing the same thing with the Paco Vazquez cartel. This is all because of Vance's cooperation. In another week, we will be doing a major sting operation to arrest the Camden and Atlantic City drug kingpin, Rosa Gomez and a few others."

JoAnn listened intently and took notes. She and Vance had already talked about everything before the meeting.

"Once these three individuals are apprehended Vance Lewis will have three days to decide if he will return to the field or sign up for the Federal Witness Protection Program. If he decides to sign up for Witness Protection, we will provide him with everything he needs for the rest of his life, including a house and a new life in the San Fernando Valley. He has been one of the longest working government informants in the Eastern District. We have benefitted greatly with Mr. Lewis's twenty years of assistance and cooperation."

JoAnn smiled and nodded her head in agreement. After the meeting, JoAnn placed her paperwork inside her briefcase and left the FBI office feeling jubilant. Vance promised her that this would probably be his last year working for the FBI. He had been considering retirement for a while now. Together they had talked about and planned to join the Witness Protection Program together and live the good life in a warm, sunny Los Angeles suburb in the San Fernando Valley. Back inside her car, JoAnn couldn't stop smiling.

"Baby, we almost at the end," she said.

8:49 A.M.

"I'll be alright baby, I'm headed to the bank now and I got Zeta with me," Queen said as she swerved her new Mercedes around Lincoln Drive. Zeta reclined in silence, looking out the window and admiring the beautiful park scenery. On the back seat was a small black Gucci backpack with $100,000 in cash neatly stacked inside. This was Queen's weekly deposit into one of her many bank accounts. Fifteen minutes later Queen pulled into the Bank of America parking lot on City Avenue.

"I'll wait in the car for you," Zeta said as she watched Queen grab the bag off the back seat.

Queen opened the door and stepped out of the car. With a hundred grand in cash in her hand, she walked across the parking lot, headed to the bank entrance. Suddenly two masked men jumped out of a tinted black van. They quickly grabbed Queen and pushed her into the van's sliding door.

On the opposite side of the parking lot, Zeta noticed all the commotion. She grabbed her loaded 9mm and rushed out of the car. With her gun aimed she started shooting at the moving van, hoping to shoot out the tires. People started running for safety, hiding behind parked cars. Standing there with a shocked look on her face Zeta watched as the van sped out of the parking lot and drove down City Avenue. Zeta then ran back over to the car and quickly drove off. She couldn't believe what had just happened. Queen had been kidnapped right in front of her eyes, and there was nothing she could have done about it.

"Y'all doing this for a snitch!" Queen shouted. "I know my father put y'all up to this but he is a snitch! An FBI informant and the man y'all work for!"

"Shut up bitch!" Magic said, pimp slapping her with the back of his hand after he and Terry removed their masks. Rosa Gomez was behind the wheel listening to every word that came out of Queen's mouth. Terry was also paying close attention to her harsh words against her father.

"He's a snitch! Fuck my father! One day he will take all y'all motherfuckers down! He's been setting up people and cooperating with the Feds for years!" Queen said.

Magic grabbed a roll of duct tape and placed a piece over Queen's mouth. For the rest of the ride, Queen sat there fuming and boiling with rage. Queen had lost all respect for her father many years ago. In a van filled with complete silence, Rosa headed towards the secret location where Vance was already waiting.

Chapter 42

"Are you serious!!?" Biggie said.

"Yes, they jumped out of a van and the shit happened so fast!" Zeta told him.

Gotti and Marvin stood in complete silence. No one could believe that Queen had been kidnapped in broad daylight.

"Did you let King know?" Zeta asked Biggie.

"Yes, I called him as soon as you told me. He's on his way back home."

The four of them were disappointed, and their feelings were all over their faces. This had been a major blow. Queen had been running the organization while King was still recovering from his gunshot wounds. They all concluded that Vance was somehow involved. He and his daughter hated each other with a passion. Zeta sat there with her head down, and tears ran from her worried eyes. She felt to blame because protecting Queen was her sole responsibility.

On the plane, back to America, King couldn't sit still. He had never felt more scared in his entire life. Hearing the terrible news about his wife being kidnapped felt like a punch to the stomach. King tried holding back his tears but, they simply wouldn't agree with him. With a bemused look and heart full of worry and confusion King sat there staring out the window crying in silence.

Chapter 43
Later that Night
Southwest Philly

Inside a two-story house on 58th & Springfield Avenue, King sat on the couch surrounded by all of his closest friends. Everyone was still in complete shock about Queen's kidnapping. King stood up from the couch and limped over to the window.

"Did anyone hear anything yet?"

"Nothing so far," Biggie answered.

"I got all of our men out searching the streets for answers," Zeta said.

"Don't worry, King we will find her, me and Marvin won't stop looking until we do," Gotti stood up and said.

"I know it's her rat ass father that's behind all of this!" King vented. "We need to find my wife!!"

"What about the cop? Maybe he can tell us something," Marvin said.

King's eyes suddenly widened, and he said, "Doc still has him?"

"Yes, and he's still alive, chained inside Doc's basement," Gotti replied. "But he ain't give up nothing yet," Biggie said.

King limped back over to the couch and sat down. "I'm not playing no more fucking games! It's time to make that fucking cop talk. Gotti, Marvin, Biggie ... I need y'all to go take care of something for me right now," King said. After telling them his plan, King watched as the three men rushed out the door.

"What do you think Zeta?" King asked.

"If that won't get the cop to talk then nothing will," Zeta replied. Zeta walked over to King and sat down beside him. "King, I'm so sorry for not keeping my eyes on her the entire time. It just happened so fast and before I knew it she was inside the van," Zeta said, as tears began running from her eyes.

King placed his arm around Zeta's shoulders and said, "I understand Zee, I know if you could've done something different you would have. Hopefully, she is still alive and her father has some sympathy for her. She is his first child. Right now, all we can do is pray," King said despondently.

Chapter 44
Henry Avenue, Manayunk

The beautiful Victorian style home was situated in the middle of the block. The street was very quiet with well-manicured lawns in front of all the houses. Most of the homeowners were retired professionals, enjoying their golden years.

Inside the large basement, Queen's naked body was strapped to a round wooden table. For hours, she had been beaten and tortured by her father and his men. Her eyes, nose, and lips were all swollen and dripping with blood.

"Bitch you gonna tell me where the fuck your husband at?" Vance screamed.

Queen looked at her father with pure hate in her eyes. "Fuck you, you snitch! You're a snitch, a rat and I will never give up my man for you!"

Vance raised his hand and smacked Queen harder than a pimp smacks his hoe. The smack was so hard that blood flew from her mouth. Rosa, Terry, Victor, and Magic all stood there watching in silence.

"Bitch, do you want to die? Die at the hands of your own father?" Vance shouted.

"Kill me! Do what you want! I'm never giving you my man's head! Never!" Queen muttered through a mouthful of blood.

Vance stood there in complete frustration. For hours, he and his men had tortured Queen and not once did she break. Suddenly he reached down and grabbed Queen's throat. "Bitch, where is that nigga?!"

"Kill me, Daddy! Kill me like you did my mother," Queen said. Vance released his grip and backed away. "Grab that plunger," Vance ordered Magic.

Magic walked over by the wall and grabbed a plunger. Then he walked over near Vance and stood by his side. "Tell me where that nigga of yours is or else you will never have his fucking child!" Vance told her.

Queen looked at her father and said, "Fuck you ya snitch ass pussy!"

"No, fuck you bitch!" Vance said, before snatching the plunger from Magic. With evil in his eyes, Vance stuck the plunger inside Queen's vagina as far as it could go. Then he began to savagely push it back and forth. Rosa placed her hand over Queen's mouth to muffle her screams.

Queen had never felt so much pain in her entire life. All she could do was lay there as her father, and his thugs took turns fucking her with the 18-inch-long plunger handle. Blood and small particles of flesh dripped out of her vagina.

"Bitch I'm personally gonna make sure that no man will ever want your ass again!" Vance told her.

After they had finally finished brutalizing Queen's inside, Vance told his men to fuck her. Magic was the first to comply with his request. After he had raped her Terry and Victor both did the same. Queen felt beyond humiliated. She was in so much pain that her entire body had become numb. As tears rolled from her eyes, all she could do is lay there watching as the three men took turns in raping her. Vance looked like the devil with an evil grin as he watched them brutalize his daughter.

"Fuck this bitch," he yelled out.

"Why don't you just kill her and end it?" Rosa said. Vance glared at Rosa and told her, "No, this is personal. She doesn't deserve to die. That's getting off easy. This bitch needs to suffer for the rest of her life. She is going to be so ugly after I'm done with her that her man is going to confuse her for a crack whore walking the streets in Kensington. That's worse than death!"

For the next hour Queen was beaten, sodomized and raped. The pain became so intense that she fainted and fell unconscious. Before Vance left the house, he looked down at his daughter's bloody and beaten body and spit on her in disgust. He felt nothing for her, and he felt totally betrayed by her. He gave everyone their orders and then left the house.

After Vance left, Rosa and Terry stepped to the side and started to whisper. As they privately discussed something, both of them watched as Victor and Magic continued to savagely rape and torture Queen's beaten and fatigued body. Moments later, Rosa and Terry walked out of the basement, leaving the two men alone with a woman that was beaten within an inch of her life.

Chapter 45
Early Tuesday
City Hall

Mayor Stan Jennings was furious. Inside his huge office the Mayor, Candice Shaw and the Chief of Police were seated at a small round table. In the past two weeks, the murder rate had sky rocketed.

"What the hell is going on out there? Cops are reported missing, murders in broad daylight, kidnappings at banks and so much more! And we have yet to get one damn arrest! My career is on the line. And if my career goes down the drain so will youse guys!" Mayor Jennings shouted.

"We are doing our best, Mayor," the Police Chief said.

"Well, Charles your best ain't good enough. You have to do more!" The Mayor replied.

"The truth is we are dealing with two major drug organizations in the city. The King organization and the Vance Lewis Cartel. The Feds are also having problems getting any type of information for an arrest. People are scared to testify, and our informants keep ending up dead. I've come to the conclusion that both sides have people on the inside working for them, or maybe they are working with the Feds. They seem to be two steps ahead of us at every turn," Candice Shaw said.

Mayor Jennings looked around the table with disappointment. This was his first term as Mayor, and he didn't want it to be his last. He worked his way up from fourteen years as a City Council member and a State Representative. He promised the citizens of Philadelphia that he would be hard on crime and do everything in his power to get rid of the drugs, murders, and violence in the city. With the elections coming up in the next year he had to show the voters that he was a man of his word.

"Get me some arrests and convictions!! Now get the fuck out of my office, both of you."

With that said Candice Shaw and the Chief of Police stood from the table and calmly walked out of the Mayor's office.

Chapter 46
West Philly

In Doc's basement, everyone stood around looking at Officer John Carter's beaten and bruised naked body. His body was thin and frail from starvation. He had lost over 100 pounds and looked as if he was on the brink of death. Still, through all the torture he endured, he refused to give up any information on Vance or members of his crew. King walked up to John and grabbed his throat.

"Look here you stupid motherfucker, tell me where Vance is at or you die!" he said.

John Carter looked at King and smirked. "You find him yourself," he struggled to say.

"You think it's a game don't you," Biggie shouted. "Nigga you're going to die for a snitch!" he added.

John Carter weakly chuckled and laid his head down. Doc and Zeta both just stood there watching. Neither one said a single word, as King and Biggie both tried to get John Carter to talk.

Suddenly Zeta's cell phone started to ring, and she answered. "Hello? Okay cool. That's good, hold on," she said. "They got em," Zeta said.

King smiled and said, "Bring it up for our friend."

Zeta pressed a button and began playing a video that Gotti sent to her phone. Then she walked over and showed John Carter. His eyes quickly widened after seeing his wife and two sons tied up inside a small room. King had remembered that he had John's driver's license, with his home address on it and other personal information he got out of his wallet. He sent Gotti and Marvin to kidnap them at their house in Northeast Philly.

"Do you think this is still a game?" King asked him. "Your wife Jane and your two sons will all die if you don't tell me what I need to know! Now where is Vance and where is my wife being held? You have one minute to tell me what I need to know or you just murdered your entire family."

For the first time since his capture, John felt defeated. As the tears started rolling down his face, he said, "Okay, I will tell you everything I know."

Chapter 47
Manayunk

Terry and Rosa were in her BMW talking. "I don't know what's going on anymore, but I'm really starting to feel like something ain't right with Vance, and he hasn't been telling us the whole truth," Rosa said.

"I feel you; it's like he's a man full of secrets," Terry replied. "Why would his daughter say that? Why would she call him a rat?"

Rosa passed Terry the letter she got from Tito and said, "Read this."

Terry started to read the letter, and when he finished he just sat there confused.

"But I don't understand, Rosa, we have been working with Vance for years, and we have never been locked up. He pays the law to leave us alone. I never heard anything bad about his name until recently."

"I'm dying to figure it out myself, but when I think about it, it's not good. Like how do all our connects keep getting locked up by the FBI? Who are those two white men that Vance be meeting up with? Why did his daughter call him a snitch? Why did Tito send me that letter? And the biggest question of them all is why hasn't Vance ever been locked up or investigated? He has been running the streets for years but everyone he started with is either dead, in prison or retired. Is he being protected by someone? Or is he just lucky?"

Terry just sat there shaking his head. "He made us all wealthy. I still have respect and loyalty for him. Maybe we are just both over thinking. Vance Lewis is a boss, a survivor, and a good man," Terry said, almost as if he was trying to convince himself.

Rosa stared deep into Terry's eyes and said, "I will always love and respect Vance, but I'm telling you this, Terry; if I ever get locked up by the FBI, Vance is responsible! He is the only person that knows everything about me. My home, my money, my drug connects and more! He is the only person that can take me down."

Terry shook his head.

"He would never do that," he said.

"I sure hope not," Rosa replied.

Chapter 48
Tuesday Night

After John told King everything he needed to know, King had Gotti and Marvin release his terrified family. They were dropped off just a few blocks away from their home. With a list of names, homes, and businesses that Gotti had gotten from King, he and Marvin gathered up a few of their most loyal men and went on a mission to find Queen.

West Philly

After King, Zeta and Biggie left, John Carter was left alone with the psychopathic Doc.

"You're all mines now," Doc said before he turned John Carter's naked body over on his stomach. "Perfect," Doc said, licking his lips and undressing. After Doc had taken off all his clothes, he grabbed a sharp, 12-inch knife off his desk. He then climbed on top of John's naked body and wrapped his right arm around his head and began cutting the back of John's neck. John laid there feeling paralyzed, unable to do anything to prevent the savage maniac from this humiliating torture. As John squirmed his body beneath him, Doc continued to cut off John's head.

Ten minutes later, John's head was detached from his lifeless body, and it fell on the floor. The sight of seeing John's head on the floor gave Doc an instant erection. Doc spread John's legs apart, and without hesitation, he slid his hard dick into John's rectum and began to savagely fuck his beheaded corpse.

A Few Hours Later

Gotti and Marvin had been driving all over the city shooting up and firebombing all of Vance's establishments, homes, and businesses. In the midst of all the chaos, they had shot and killed five of Vance's men. Tonight, they were on a mission to kill anything connected to the Vance organization. Fire trucks and police cars were flying around all over the city. King told his crew not to stop until every one of Vance's properties were burnt to the ground and Queen was found.

Chapter 49
Wynnewood, PA

King sat down on the sofa and closed his eyes. Being in his home alone felt strange and made him very uncomfortable. He sat there feeling lost without Queen's presence. The war with Vance was beginning to take its toll on him, and without Queen by his side, King felt dead inside. In the quietness of his home tears began to run from his eyes. His soul mate was gone and no one knew where she was. Even after getting all the info out of John Carter his street team had still been unable to find her.

Northeast Philadelphia

"What's wrong babe?" JoAnn asked Vance after noticing the distant look on his face. "Are you okay?"

"No, not really, but I will be," Vance replied. As his text messages continued to go off Vance ignored them and turned off his cell phone.

"You know you can talk to me about anything."

"I know babe, but it's about my daughter, Queen. I had to do something to her today. I had to teach her a lesson for betraying me!!!"

JoAnn looked at Vance and asked, "Did you kill her?"

"No, but after what I did and had my men do to her, she's going to wish she was dead."

"Well, she married your enemy and tried to have you murdered," JoAnn said, as she began to rub Vance's neck.

"She's still my daughter, my first child."

"She hates you, Vance, always did and always will."

"I know, that's why I want her to suffer for the rest of her life. Every time she looks in a mirror or sees a newborn baby I want her to think about me," Vance fumed.

JoAnn laid next to Vance and didn't say a word. She knew his capabilities and never would dare question his decisions.

"I think I'm done with all this shit! I'm ready to retire from the game. So once all of this is over I'm done, and I will be ready to start a new life with you, 3000 miles away from this shithole city in warm, sunny LA," Vance said, as he rolled over on top of JoAnn's naked body.

"And I can't wait," JoAnn smiled.

Chapter 50
Early Wednesday Morning

The black van pulled up and parked near the Philadelphia Art Museum. A small community of homeless people were situated behind the building. They had been sleeping on benches and living in makeshift cardboard homes. They were people of all races and religions who had fallen on hard times and were currently at their lowest point in life.

Suddenly the sliding doors on the van opened and two men quickly tossed Queen's bruised, beaten, naked body to the cold ground. Then the van quickly sped off. A small group of homeless people gathered around Queen's body. A broken plunger stick was still inserted inside her vagina and was covered in blood.

A homeless man named Gary placed his blanket over Queen's naked body and tried his best to comfort her. "Are you ok? What's your name?"

Queen didn't respond. She was too badly beaten and too frail to say or do anything.

"I'm going to get you some help, just hold on young lady," Gary said. Before rushing off to get Queen some help, he placed his jacket under her head and said, "I got you! Just try to stay alive for me."

As Gary ran off for help the group of homeless people all gathered around Queen's body to help keep her warm from the cold. Twenty minutes later an ambulance and a police car pulled up to the scene. The EMT's quickly ran over to Queen's body.

"We have to get her to the hospital now! Or she won't make it!" one of the men said.

Moments later Queen's body was being placed inside of the ambulance.

"Can I go with her?" Gary asked.

It was obvious that he was very concerned about the young woman.

"Sure, come on," the man told him. Gary got inside of the ambulance before it sped off down the street. Inside the ambulance, Gary sat back crying and praying for a woman that he didn't know. He knew that it was the right thing to do. Even though he had been homeless for years, he was still human.

Chapter 51
8th & Arch
Three Days Later

Vance was furious beyond words. After finding out that most of his businesses had been burned to the ground, he was incensed. He had also lost five of his top men from late night shootings. At the moment, the war between Vance and King was dead even. Both sides had suffered major losses.

Vance walked down the street and got inside the waiting car. Terry was waiting in the driver's seat.

"How did the meeting with your two business partners go?" Terry asked, before driving off.

"It went very well," Vance smiled.

Terry nodded his head and continued to drive. For the rest of the ride he didn't say too much because he was deep in thought. He considered the conversations that he had been having with Rosa. He didn't want to believe that all this time he had been working for an FBI informant. He had been with Vance for over ten years. Just the thought of Vance being a snitch upset his stomach. Then Terry realized where he was parked while he waited for Vance. He was parked just a few blocks away from the FBI Federal Building on 6th and Arch Street. All he could do was shake his head and speculate.

West Philadelphia

A dark colored Buick slowly pulled up in front of the 16th Police District on Lancaster Avenue. The window rolled down, and a green plastic trash bag was tossed near the front entrance. The car then sped off down the street. Inside the bag was the decapitated head of Officer John Carter and his bloody police badge. His eyes, ears, and nose were all removed from his face. Back inside the car Gotti and Marvin were both laughing. They hated cops, so dropping off one of their heads wasn't work at all. It was pure excitement!

~~~

Inside his kitchen, Doc was sitting at the table feasting on parts of John Carter's flesh. As he sat there eating, he looked at the small glass jar that he had filled with vinegar and eight eyeballs inside of it.
~~~

Chapter 52
Wynnewood, PA

King was lying on the couch when his cell phone started ringing.

"Hello?"

"Baby it's me, come get me," Queen said.

"Where are you!?!" King responded with excitement in his voice.

"I'm at Hahnemann Hospital, room 340, come get me please!" Queen told him.

"I'm on my way now!" King said before the phone call ended. King put on his boots and jacket and rushed out the door. He quickly called Zeta and Biggie and told them to meet him at Hahnemann Hospital.

A half hour later, King, Biggie, and Zeta were all rushing through the hospital doors.

When King walked into Queen's room, he couldn't believe his watery eyes. Queen was lying in bed with bandages covering her face and IV's in her arms. It was obvious that she had been beaten and tortured, almost to the brink of death. Sitting in a chair in the corner of the room was her homeless friend Gary. He had never left her side the entire time she was there.

"Who are you?" King asked.

"He is my friend. He saved my life," Queen said in a low voice.

Zeta and Biggie stood there while King leaned down and hugged his wife. He was just happy that she was still alive. His prayers had reached God's ears, and his Queen was back in his life.

For the next half hour, Queen told them everything that had happened. King sat back in tears, listening as his wife told him all about her horrific ordeal. When a doctor walked into the room, he asked to talk to King and Queen alone. Zeta and Biggie stepped out of the room and waited in the hallway.

"You have to leave also," the doctor told Gary.

"Give me a few minutes Gary," Queen said to her homeless friend. He hesitantly got up out of his chair and sadly walked out of the room.

"What's up Doc? Is there something wrong?" King asked with a worried expression.

The doctor looked at both of them and said, "I'm sorry to say, but I have some very disturbing news," he told them.

"Just keep it real with us," King said.

"Mr. Smith, your wife had to have major surgery on her cervix, uterus, and rectum. She experienced some major genital injuries. She has a large tear in her labia, and stitches in her anus. Her uterus is so severely damaged that she may never be able to bear children. Besides that, she lost a lot of blood, her nose is broken, and her right retina was damaged. She also sustained a fractured left wrist, and she has rib injuries. She is truly lucky to be alive. If not for her friend Gary, she would have surely bled to death and died from her injuries."

King sat there almost frozen, feeling hurt, confused and angry all at the same time.

"We have to get her out of here Doc, we can't stay here," King said.

"But we still have to run a few more tests, and detectives want to talk to her in the morning."

"Doc we are not staying here!" King said with authority.

Zeta, Biggie, and Gary all walked back into the room.

"Please, she needs rest and the proper care for her injuries."

"Don't worry, she is going to get the very best care money can buy," King said, as he and Gary picked up Queen and sat her in a wheelchair. The doctor stood back and watched as King covered Queen in a blanket and rolled her out of the room. He didn't even try to prevent them from leaving. It was plain to see that King wasn't a man to play with, and challenging his authority would not be wise.

Outside the hospital, King and Gary helped Queen get into his tinted black Suburban. Then Zeta and Biggie got into their cars and waited to follow them home.

"Gary is coming with us," Queen struggled to say. King didn't question her decision, he just looked at Gary and said,

"Get in Gary. You're coming home with us."

With a big smile plastered on his face, Gary climbed into the Suburban and closed the door.

Chapter 53
Ridge Avenue
One Week Later

Dimplez pulled up and parked Biggie's brand new Audi in front of her apartment. Biggie had been letting her use his car to pick the girls up from school and to take her stuff to her new apartment. Dimplez had gotten her and the girls a new luxury apartment on City Avenue. Today was their last day at their old apartment, and Dimplez couldn't wait to move away from North Philly and start a new life with Biggie and her twin daughters.

Inside the apartment Dimplez helped her daughters with their homework, they watched a Disney movie, and she gave them a bubble bath after they all had dinner. When the girls were asleep Dimplez took a shower then got into bed. She was excited that this was her last night on Ridge Avenue. Her new life would be starting in a few hours.

As she lay in bed talking on the phone with Biggie, she suddenly heard a loud crashing sound come through the front window.

"Hold on baby!" Dimplez said, as she jumped up out of bed and ran out of her bedroom.

Dimplez was surprised to see her living room was engulfed in flames and smoke. Someone had tossed a Molotov cocktail through the window and ran off. She quickly ran into her daughter's room and got both of them. Then the three of them ran out of the back door to safety.

"Somebody tried to kill us!!" Dimplez said to Biggie on the phone.

"I'm on my way!" Biggie said before the line went dead.

Dimplez and her twin daughters stood there in tears watching as their apartment was engulfed in smoke and flames. Luckily, they had already moved most of their belongings to the new apartment.

Twenty minutes later, Biggie pulled up with Gotti and Marvin. The first person Biggie noticed was Lakisha, the girl from across the street. There was something about her that didn't sit well with him. He noticed her staring at him a few times before. He gave Lakisha a hard stare then ran over to comfort his crying girlfriend and her twins.

As the firemen were putting out the fire, they all got inside of Marvin's truck and he drove off into the night. Twenty minutes later, Marvin pulled up in front of the Lowes Hotel in Center City. After checking Dimplez and her daughters into the hotel, he promised to pick them up in the morning and take them to their new home.

"Let's go back and get my car," Biggie told Marvin. When Biggie got back to his car he saw Lakisha standing on her step holding a newborn baby. Seeing the smirk on her face made him realize that Lakisha had something to do with the firebombing.

"What's up Biggie?" Gotti asked.

"I need y'all to follow me. I have to take care of something," Biggie said before he got into his car and drove off.

Northeast Philadelphia

Vance sat inside the tinted Crown Vic talking to FBI agents Tony and Lucas.

"Paco Vazquez and Rosa Gomez will both be arrested in two days. The indictments were signed, and now we will have our arrest teams in Atlantic City and Miami ready to apprehend them both," Agent Lucas said.

Vance just sat there speechless nodding his head. He knew that this day had to come soon and there was nothing he could do about it. Rosa and Paco both had to go so he could move on with his life in the Federal Witness Protection Program.

"As far as Terry and Victor, they will both be spared for the time being. They are small fish in a big pond," Agent Tony said.

"So y'all are not going to arrest them?"

"No. Not yet. We don't want to make things too obvious. Plus, the Bureau knows that they have both been working in your organization for years. They allowed it to happen so that you could succeed in the game. We might even let them continue to stay out here and just watch them from a distance. We have our eyes on a few others as well. That's what we do; let them stay out here and get big, and then we take down their entire organization. These drug dealing criminals really think they're in charge when the truth is the Feds know everything that's going on in the streets," Agent Lucas said.

Chapter 54
Ridge Avenue

Lakisha Jones stood on the front steps watching as the firemen put out the last part of the fire. After the fire had subsided and the small crowd of people dispersed she walked back into her house. Lakisha then took out her cell phone and made a call.

"Hello," a voice said.

"Her and her kids got out alive, and that lil' midget nigga wasn't there. It was a false alarm, she was driving his car, not him," she said into the phone.

While Lakisha continued to talk on the phone, revealing her involvement with the fire, she never noticed the small figure beneath her bed. Holding a 9mm with an attached silencer Biggie lay still under the bed. His intuition had been right about Lakisha all along. After Lakisha ended the call, she laid back on the bed and started to breastfeed her four-month-old baby boy.

Biggie rolled over and stood up pointing his gun and Lakisha's head.

"Bitch you should've minded your own business!" he said, before putting two bullets in her head. He watched as Lakisha's lifeless body slumped in the bed. Her newborn child continued to suck on his dead mother's breast. Biggie walked through the house and out the back door, the same door that he had picked the lock to enter. Parked out back was Marvin's Chevy Tahoe. When Biggie got back inside he said, "Okay, y'all can take me back to my car, it's done."

"You take care of the baby too?" Gotti asked as Marvin pulled off.

"Naw, I decided to let the lil' bastard live. It ain't his fault that his nosy mom couldn't mind her own business. That's why I put her mind on her pillow," Biggie laughed.

"What's next on the agenda?" Marvin asked.

"We still need to find that rat Vance and his crew. What they did to Queen was horrible!! I heard that she's been going through it and dealing with PTSD. It will be a while before we get our Queen back," Biggie sorrowfully said. "A long while."

Chapter 55
Early the Next Morning

Magic couldn't believe his eyes, when he saw that the Police had Lakisha's apartment taped off. A small group of people stood about in complete shock. Lakisha was well liked in the hood, and people had seemed to gravitate towards her. A neighbor had found Lakisha dead in bed with her baby boy crying next to her. Now a small fleet of news vans and reporters stood outside trying to find answers about who would murder a single mother that had been well liked by so many.

"Did this have anything to do with last night's fire?" A reporter asked a neighbor. "Did she have any enemies ... do you think it was a robbery gone wrong?" were some of the questions that reporters asked.

Magic sadly walked away and got back inside Terry's car. In the past few months, he had lost his mother, brother and now Lakisha, his ex-girlfriend. Magic knew who the responsible people were. In the silence of Terry's car, he made a personal vow to one day avenge all their deaths.

South Philadelphia

Johnny Marino and Chow-men had sat back and listened to the anonymous call a dozen times. The message on the phone had come from a private number a few days earlier. Johnny pressed play on his cell phone and listened to the call again: "I know who y'all want and I can help y'all get him. Just give me a little time and I will bring him to y'all. Just have my money when I do. Talk to y'all soon."

"Do you think it's real, or another fake call?" Chow asked.

"I'm not sure, but whoever it is, he sounds real and very confident. We have to be on point. Also, it could be a setup. Just like our brothers were set up and murdered," Johnny replied.

"Well if it's another fake call or hoax they will wish it wasn't, but if it is real, he has a million and a half dollars waiting for him. Like I've said many times, Vance can't hide forever and money will make a man's own mother turn against him," Chow said, with a smirk on his face. "Vance is a dead man walking," he added.

New Brunswick, New Jersey, 6:58 A.M.

A swarm of FBI, DEA, and members of the New Brunswick Police Department surrounded the penthouse suite. They had been given orders to take Rosa Gomez down and bring her in alive. She had been indicted on a group of charges, ranging from drug distribution and possession to extortion, kidnapping, and murder.

As Rosa slept peacefully in bed, surrounded by two attractive Latina women, a loud booming sound awoke them from all from their sleep. With infrared beams glowing in the darkness the Feds ran in and out of every room until they came across a terrified Rosa. Rosa and her two girlfriends were all quickly apprehended and placed in an FBI van.

In the back of the van, Rosa sat in total silence. She was still in complete shock. As she sat with a stoic face a vision of Vance entered her mind. She didn't have to ask anyone anything because she knew who was responsible. If Vance wasn't arrested too, then he had to be the person guilty for her downfall. Since receiving Tito's letter, she had been deeply worried.

About forty-five minutes later, the FBI van arrived in Philadelphia, where Rosa would be processed. Sitting inside a private cell, Rosa was given a pen, pad, and an envelope. She had to get a very important letter out.

Miami, FL

Once again Paco Vazquez had secretly snuck into the US in disguise. He and a close associate walked into the lobby of the Hilton hotel. As they approached the elevators a swarm of undercover FBI and DEA agents quickly engaged on them. Paco Vazquez couldn't believe it. He had thoroughly taken certain precautions to avoid US authorities.

As a small crowd gathered around Paco and his friend, they were handcuffed, read their rights and escorted from the premises. Inside the FBI van, Paco knew that he would never see his freedom again. For years, he and his cartel had been on the FBI's Top Ten Most Wanted list. As the world spun around him, Paco felt confused and betrayed. In the silence of the van, Paco tallied up a list of people that could've been responsible for his arrest.

Chapter 56
Two Weeks Later

With the help of his good friend Luther Dynasty, King had gotten Queen some of the best medical care in the world. Luther had personally flown in the top plastic surgeons from Austria and Japan to reconstruct Queen's face. Luther had also reached out to the vaginoplasty surgeon at the University of Pennsylvania.

So, for the past few weeks, Queen had been recovering from multiple surgeries. King had also paid for one of the top psychologists in Philly to come help Queen deal with her PTSD. At night, she would awaken from nightmares screaming out loud and drenched in sweat. King had paid for the best medical care money could buy, twenty-four-hour service, with nurses and doctors working around the clock.

While Queen had been recovering, her friend, Gary, had never left her side. In a few weeks, they had created a close bond and relationship. To make Queen happy, King let Gary move into one of the spare bedrooms. He also had Gary cleaned up and checked out medically for any symptoms or diseases. Gary had turned out clean. He had just been a man that had fallen hard on his luck.

Without Queen's knowledge, King had Gary secretly investigated by a top private investigator. He found out that Gary's real name was Gary Mathews. Ironically, he had once been a former bodyguard for Will Smith, Patti LaBelle, and Allen Iverson. At 54 years-old Gary was still in peak shape, muscular and athletic and his mind was sharp. He was an avid chess player and book reader. Standing at 6 feet 3 he had an imposing figure that accentuated his dark black complexion.

Gary had eventually grown on King. That's why King didn't mind him being around his wife. In the meantime, King and his crew were still out every day searching for Vance or any members of his organization. King wouldn't stop until all of them paid the ultimate price for what they had done to Queen.

Chapter 57

In his backyard, King was shooting jump shots on the basketball court. With each make or miss, Biggie retrieved the ball and passed it back to him. As King continued to shoot baskets, the psychologist walked outside and approached him.

"Wassup Dr. Riley?" King asked.

"I wanted to talk to you about your wife," he said.

King passed the ball to Biggie and said, "Talk to me."

"I think it would be a good thing if Queen went away for a while to one of the top health and wellness resorts in America. I believe it would help her out tremendously, on an emotional, spiritual, and physical level. She needs inner healing and spiritual discovery. She's been severely traumatized, and I truly believe this will help her."

"What does Queen want?" King asked.

"She said it's up to you."

King looked into Dr. Riley's eyes and said, "Okay, when can she leave?"

"Tomorrow morning. I can have everything in order and she can be on a plane by 6 am."

"Where is this place located?" King asked.

"It's called the Spirit Rock Meditation Center, and it's located in California just outside of Los Angeles. It's less than a resort and more of an educational institute. It's dedicated to the teachings of the dharma or 'the deepest truth of life.' Silent retreats are their specialty, but they do so much more."

King agreed to let Queen go away for 30 days. Even though he didn't want to leave her side, deep down he knew it was the best thing to do. For protection, he had also paid for Gary to go with her.

After Biggie left, King walked upstairs to the master bedroom. Queen was sitting up in the bed. The TV was on and she was sipping a cup of hot green tea.

"How do you feel?" King asked

"I'm feeling better babe," Queen replied.

King said, "Gary is packing and getting all your things together for your flight in the morning."

Gazing into his eyes, Queen said, "Thanks love."

King reached over and hugged his wife. "I'm gonna miss you."

"I'm going to miss you too," Queen said, smiling. "But I will be back before you know it."

"Just go and get well, I need my rider back," King beamed.

Chapter 58
A Few Days Later
Mt. Erie

Terry sat inside his car deep in thought. For the past few weeks, his mind had been confused and clouded with emotions. Nothing had affected him more than Rosa's arrest by the Feds. She had been one of his closest friends and true allies. Suddenly, the car door opened and Vance got inside. Vance sat down holding a large black Adidas sports bag.

"Here's your money Terry. I already paid Victor and Magic," he said.

Terry unzipped the bag and looked inside at all the stacks of cash. Before Vance got out of the car, he asked him, "Did you hear from Rosa yet? Did she tell you what happened? What's the deal with her?"

After a long sigh, Vance looked at Terry and said, "No, I haven't heard anything from her yet." Vance added, "Right now, it's just best to be cautious and see what happens next. She will reach out to us. I just hope she knows how to keep her mouth closed."

Terry was shocked to hear Vance say those words.

"Rosa ain't no snitch! She would never tell on us or anyone. She is and has always been a stand-up chick," Terry replied with seriousness in his voice.

Vance gave Terry a hard stare and said, "How do we know she can be trusted? Why haven't we heard anything from her in weeks? What if she's working with the FBI to take us down? In this game, no one can be trusted. I'm the only person you can trust Terry! Me! I took you and your twin brother off the streets and put y'all under my wing! I made you more money in your lifetime than you would have ever seen! The hell with Rosa right now. She might be our newest enemy for all we know," Vance said before he angrily got out of the car.

Terry sat back in total silence, feeling lost, confused and betrayed. Still, he could never see Rosa as being a rat or ever working as an informant. Like himself, Rosa was a rat killer. A person that hated authorities.

After starting up the car, Terry opened the door and Magic got inside.

"Wassup next?" Magic asked.

"Let's go kill someone!" Terry replied.

Chapter 59
Terre Haute, Indiana

Inside a secret location at the Terre Haute Federal Prison Rosa sat alone inside her small cell. The Bureau of Prisons (BOP) had orders to place Rosa and a few other high profile convicts inside the Communications Management Unit (CMU). All CMU's were run by the heads in Washington, DC. Once you were housed in a CMU facility, there were severe restrictions on phone calls, mail and visits. The CMU's were so private that there was no info on the BOP website about any special unit at Terre Haute even existing. The truth was that the Bush administration had quietly opened CMU's at numerous Federal prisons across the nation. CMU's mostly housed Arab and Muslim American terrorists, drug lords, spies and foreign criminals plotting against the United States.

For weeks Rosa had no contact with the outside world. The only letter that she had managed to get out was the letter she had written to Terry after first getting arrested. She wasn't even sure if he had ever received it. Rosa had yet to talk to any representative from the BOP or her attorney. She was considered a major threat to the US, helping to flood the streets of America with drugs from foreign countries. So, like many others, Rosa's arrest was done with the highest secrecy.

While she waited, the government could do as they pleased. Homeland Security had considered her a major terrorist. The goal was to break her down slowly. Dressed in a bright orange jumpsuit, Rosa sat on the bunk and cried. In a few weeks, her life had changed dramatically. The Feds had frozen all her bank accounts and assets and seized all her properties. She was now a scared woman with nothing. No friends, money or property to call her own. The sad part was that the man she had been loyal to for over seven years was the person responsible for all she was going through. In the silence of her cell, all she could do was listen to her tears fall to the floor.

Chapter 60
Chestnut Hill, PA

King, Biggie, and Zeta sat at a large wooden table with stacks of bills laid out. Two large suitcases had already been placed against the wall, with two million dollars inside each one. King had changed his entire business around. He had all his street workers start working with untraceable cell phones and using secret locations for drop offs and deliveries. With the help of Luther Dynasty, King had purchased an old church and a cemetery in North Philadelphia. Each of them had come in handy for his lucrative drug business.

"Any word yet?" King asked Biggie?

"Nothing yet on Vance or Terry, but word on the streets is that Rosa got knocked by the Feds a couple weeks ago."

King nodded his head and said, "I heard about that, and I had Roscoe check into it to see if there was any truth to it. So far, he can't find anything on Rosa Gomez, and that's strange. Something is going on and I'm positive Vance's rat ass is behind it!"

Zeta sat there shaking her head. "If Vance really is an informant that has been working with the FBI for twenty years then he must be one of the biggest rats in history. How can a person survive on the streets that long?"

"By working with the Feds and other rats! The feds let Sammy The Bull get out after committing over 20 murders! They don't care. As long as you're working with them, they will keep you out here on the streets. The game is fucked up!" Biggie vented out in anger.

"Well fuck em all! I want Vance out here so I can kill the motherfucker for what he did to my wife. Because of him, Queen can never have a child! I will never be a father. They will all die for what they did to my woman. Every last one of them will die for the pain Queen suffered," King said.

The three of them then finished counting all the money.

Chapter 61
Spirit Rock Meditation Center
Los Angeles, CA

After only a few days on the compound, Queen and Gary settled into their new surroundings. Queen was really enjoying the enlightening experience and a chance to get away from all the turmoil and violence back in Philly. Her wounds and surgeries were all healing well, and from the outside, a person couldn't imagine all the pain she had endured.

As the two of them walked down a dirt path, Queen paused and said, "Gary, I need you to do a big favor for me. I need you to leave and go check something out."

Gary nodded his head and said, "Whatever you want or need me to do."

"I need to find out something very important. It's been troubling me for a while now. Don't worry; I will cover for you here while you're away," Queen told him.

After Queen had told Gary what she needed him to do, he packed some belongings and snuck away from the Center. A couple of hours later Gary was at the Los Angeles International Airport boarding a flight to Baltimore.

Northeast Philly

After just finishing a pleasing oral sex performance JoAnn crawled up and laid on Vance's chest. "Babe, how do you feel?"

"I feel good," Vance said, running his hand through her hair.

"Can I ask you something?" she said.

"Anything love," Vance replied.

"Do you think anyone is suspicious of Rosa's disappearance?"

"I don't think so, Terry asked me about her, but I had to set him straight."

"I just was wondering that's all", JoAnn said. "I know she was well liked by all in your crew."

Vance sat up in the bed and said, "Don't worry, everything is cool. No one will ever find out that I'm involved with Rosa, Tito, Paco, or any of the many others that I helped to put behind bars. In another week, all of this shit will be past us and we will be long gone!" Vance smiled.

Chapter 62
Early the Next Morning
King of Prussia, PA

The tinted black Mercedes Benz pulled into the crowded KOP Mall parking lot and parked near the front entrance. Then King stepped out of the car and walked over to a nearby Chevy Suburban. When King opened the door and stepped inside, Scarface and his partner Quincy were patiently waiting for him.

"Wassup Cuz?" King asked.

"I'm good, what's going on with you? And what happened to Queen?" Face asked.

"She was kidnapped, but everything is good now. I got her back, and now she's away recuperating," King replied.

After King told Face the entire story Face sat back speechless.

"You're lucky King. It could easily have been a lot worse. You need to eliminate your problem as soon as possible."

"But Vance ain't been easy to find and get. My boys are out looking for him every day." King said.

"Well just stay focused and no more slip ups or close calls."

"I will, Face. I changed my entire business around, and things are going much better."

Face looked at his younger cousin and said, "Remember what I told you. No credit cards in your name, homes, or cars. Information is powerful. It can make you or break you. Vance is being protected, that's why all his information is sealed and can't be traced. He has to be a top government informant because my people can't find a single thing on him. The Feds love their rats. So, you need to cover your ass and use as little information as possible. The less info they have on you, the harder it is for them to get you."

"I understand, Face. I've been working with my lawyers, accountants and Luther Dynasty." King smiled.

"Good, just get your problems fixed and get that rat out of here," Face told him.

Chapter 63
Park Heights, Baltimore, MD

Inside a rented Ford Taurus Gary sat back taking pictures of a small row house. He watched as a few people went in and out of the home. As he sat there taking pictures and texting notes into his cell phone, he sent everything back to Queen. An hour later, Gary was headed to the airport to join Queen back at the Center. He had a lot to tell her and Queen couldn't wait to hear it all in person.

27th Street, North Philadelphia

The church van pulled up and parked in back of the old Baptist church. Three men, dressed in dark suits, got out carrying boxes and a large duffel bag. A church orderly quickly escorted them down to a private section in the basement. Inside the boxes and duffle bags were kilos of cocaine.

The house of God was being used for so much more than worship. It had also been a secret stash house for drugs, guns, and money. King had recently purchased the old property from his friend Luther Dynasty. He had also purchased a cemetery near Ridge Avenue. King's street teams were no longer using street corners and drug houses to move product. They were now working out of the church to throw off their enemies and local authorities.

For the past two weeks business had been extremely good. They had moved over 500 kilos, 100 guns and over $2 million in cash, all through the church. On Sundays, King would have his church employees feed the local homeless and pass out church pamphlets to the neighborhood. He didn't want anyone to become suspicious of what was truly going on behind the church walls. All the old benches, the pulpit, office floors, and curtains were replaced with newer items and furniture. King had also bought three new church vans and Bibles for all the members. And the $2,500 a week made his new pastor turn a blind eye to everything. He asked no questions at all, and that's the way King liked it.

After the men had dropped off the drugs, they got back into the church van and drove away.

Chapter 64
City Line Avenue

Inside her new bedroom, Dimplez's naked body was spread out on the large king sized bed. Once again, she and Biggie had just finished an intense round of hard, aggressive sex. Biggie walked out of the bathroom and climbed back in bed to join her. Since meeting each other sex had been non-stop. Dimplez was everything he ever wanted in a woman. She was beautiful and smart and one hell of a cook. Biggie was pleased with his choice and happy to have a loyal woman by his side.

When Biggie lay next to her, Dimplez kissed him on the lips and asked, "Do you fear anything?"

Biggie smiled and said, "Yes, I'm human. Why do you ask?"

"Because you seem so fearless like nothing bothers you. I was just wondering that's all."

"Well, I have fears like everyone else," Biggie replied.

"Like what?"

"I fear God. I fear my friends becoming disloyal. I fear being broke," he smiled.

"You're funny."

"I'm serious. I came up hard. Poverty is all I've ever known. My mother is dead; my father is serving a life sentence. All I have ever known was pain and poverty. That's till I met my partner, King. He was one of the top basketball players in America, and he promised me that one day he would take me to the top with him. Not once did he ever lie or look down at me as less than a man. He is the one person that I fear losing," Biggie said sincerely.

Dimplez smiled and kissed Biggie on the lips. "Well, hopefully, one day you will feel that same way about me because I fear losing you. You saved me and my girls and I will always love and respect you for that."

Chapter 65
North Philly

Roscoe had thoroughly gathered all the information needed from John Carter's cell phone. He had come up with a list of names, addresses, cars, and businesses. John Carter's cell phone had contained a treasure trove of personal information that King desperately needed.

Roscoe sent all the info to a secret email he personally made for King. King was the only person with access to open and read its contents. When King received, and read the secret email, he was very pleased with all that Roscoe found out. Even King was surprised to discover so much info on his enemies. King quickly called all of his top people for an important meeting. They were all to meet at the church in two hours.

West Philly

The 48 Laws of Power by Robert Greene had always been one of Terry's favorite books. As he sat back reading it, he had an epiphany. For years, murder, death, drugs, blood, and money had consumed him. In the midst of it all, he had lost his twin brother and so many of his close friends to prison and death. As he sat there engrossed in the book, Terry heard the mail slot on the door open and a few pieces of mail drop to the floor. He put the book down and got up from his seat. Terry walked over and picked up the mail from the floor. When he saw the name Rosa Gomez, #62699-066 he quickly opened the small letter.

Terry stood there reading the letter in complete shock. When he finished, he called Magic and Victor and told them to come to his house. Something wasn't right, and Terry was determined to get down to the bottom of it and hopefully find some answers to his many questions. As he waited for Victor and Magic to show up he sat back down and finished reading one of his favorite chapters in the book -- Law #2: Never put too much trust in friends.

Chapter 66
Three Days Later

Queen had never felt better in her life. Her spirits were high, and it was obvious that she was starting to feel like her old self again. Her surgeries were healing well, but more importantly, her emotional and spiritual levels were all positive. The vacation was much needed, not only for Queen but for her good friend and bodyguard, Gary, as well. No one would have known that just a few weeks earlier Gary was a homeless man living in a makeshift cardboard home.

For hours they would talk about life, the past, and future. They had confided in each other with many of their most personal and deepest secrets. Secretly, Queen wished she had a father like Gary: someone who would protect her and place her life before his own. She had always been attracted to strong Black men. That's why she married King.

A few times at night she would sometimes lay in bed and cry. The thought of never having a child had deeply bothered her. She didn't just want a child; she wanted King's child.

In the meantime, Queen knew that she had to get herself back together. Her husband needed her and it was imperative that she go home to Philly stronger, wiser and more focused than ever before.

Downtown Philadelphia

"This is a list of all those properties you asked me for," Luther said, passing a white sheet of paper to King. "I had my secretary gather all the information for you."

King looked at the paper and smiled.

"Thanks, Luther."

"How is the old church and cemetery working for you?"

"The church is doing well, and I'm preparing the cemetery now," King laughed.

After a brief conversation, King left Luther's office and got back in the SUV with Biggie, Gotti, and Marvin.

"Okay fellas, I have everything we need. Tonight, it's going down. I want them all," King said.

Chapter 67
FBI Office
6th & Arch Street

Candice Shaw was incensed as she sat back listening to the FBI director. As he continued to speak, she finally stood up and said, "Why can't I get any information on Vance Lewis? Why am I constantly being refused his classified files? His name has been coming up for years and not once has the FBI helped the City of Philadelphia with his investigation. Why is he being protected? This man and his crew of savages have been terrorizing the city of Philadelphia for decades. He has left a bloody path of murder and chaos!"

Everyone around the round table looked at Candice with hard stares. Then suddenly it had become clear. "Vance Lewis is an informant? Is that what it is? He's working with the FBI?"

One of the men walked over to Candice and said, "That's information we are unable to disclose. As we told you so many times, Vance Lewis is our responsibility, and we don't need any interference by you or Philadelphia authorities."

With that said the meeting ended and everyone left the conference room.

Inside her car, Candice sat in the driver's seat totally confused. The realization that Vance Lewis was an informant had finally set in. "Now I understand," she said to herself as she started her car and slowly pulled onto Broad Street.

49th & Parkside, West Philadelphia

Inside a small warehouse Vance, Terry, Victor, and Magic stood around a large stack of cocaine. Over 500 kilos were in the middle of the floor.

"We run this city!" Vance said. "I promised to make y'all rich, and that's what I did!"

As he continued to speak everyone stood in silence, intensely observing him. They let Vance have the floor doing what he did best. When Vance finished his speech, Terry walked up to him with a serious expression. He then passed Vance the letter he received from Rosa.

"What's this?"

"Just read it," Terry said.

Vance stood there reading the letter. After he finished he crumbled it up and threw the balled-up letter on the floor.

"You believe that bullshit? Are you going to trust that bitch over me?" Vance shouted.

With tears in his eyes, Terry pulled out a loaded .40 caliber and pointed it at Vance's head.

"Rosa had no reason to lie on you. The FBI has arrested everyone that's been around you. All of your drug connections are locked up doing lengthy sentences."

"Are you locked up? Are any of y'all in prison?" Vance said. "I saved you and your twin brother, and I made sure that nothing ever happened to y'all under my watch. I never once turned my back on any of y'all." Vance looked at Victor and Magic and watched as they stood there with stoic expressions.

"Stop it, Vance! Just stop it! We know what you've been doing this whole time. We also know that those two partners of yours are FBI agents, and your own daughter was telling us the truth about you. You're a snitch! You have been setting up drug dealers for years!" Terry shouted out.

Vance fell to his knees and said, "I'm not a snitch! You just don't understand! Please, Terry, don't do this! Don't do me like this; you're like a son to me!"

Terry looked into Vance's watery eyes and said, "I could never hurt you. I live by a code of respect and loyalty. But this is something I can't allow to go any further."

Then Terry looked in Magic's direction and nodded his head. With that signal, Magic took out his 9mm pistol and walked over to Vance. Without hesitation, he pointed it and squeezed the trigger three times. Each bullet went right into Vance's head. His lifeless body slumped hard to the ground, and a pool of blood quickly formed around his head.

As Terry and Magic stood there speechless, Victor ran outside to the van and quickly returned with a black body bag. They placed Vance's corpse inside the body bag, then put him in the back of the van.

"Victor we will all meet up later, I have some other business to take care of," Terry told him.

When Victor got into his car and drove off, Magic and Terry drove off in the van.

"Are you okay?" Magic asked him.

"I'm good. The world is always a better place when a rat is exposed and terminated," Terry replied.

Magic nodded his head and continued to drive to their next destination in South Philly.

A Few Hours Later

JoAnn Morgan nervously waited with FBI agents Tony and Lucas. They had been calling and texting Vance's cell phone for hours. Today was the day Vance was supposed to sign his official release papers as a special government informant and prepare himself for the Federal Witness Protection Program. The government had already purchased him and JoAnn a beautiful home in California surrounded by land and tall trees. They all had known something was terribly wrong. Vance had never missed a call or failed to return a text message from his phone.

"Something isn't right! I'm telling you," JoAnn cried. "You guys need to go find him! He's in trouble somewhere; I can just feel it."

"Where is the last place he said he was going?" Agent Tony asked.

"He didn't say. He just got dressed and left the house this morning."

"Well, we have our agents out searching for him right now," Agent Lucas assured her. "Right now, all we can do is wait."

"Just go home and wait. He could've lost his phone or misplaced it," Agent Tony said.

With tears freely flowing JoAnn walked out of the office and down the long hallway. Her mind was racing with thoughts, and her stomach was rumbling with discomfort. Back inside her car, JoAnn couldn't hold it any longer. She yelled out as loud as she could and slammed her fist down on the steering wheel.

"Where the hell are you?" she screamed. "I need you Vance; I need you!"

Chapter 68
Later That Night
Southwest Philly

Zeta and Biggie sat in a car watching as members of Vance's street crew went in and out of a small house. On the opposite side of town, Gotti and Marvin were doing the same thing. While other members of King's crew were all out secretly watching homes owned and operated by the Vance organization, they were all waiting for King to give them the final word.

With the help of Roscoe and Luther, King had gathered all the information he needed to eliminate Vance's entire organization. He had a list of names, numbers, and properties. King was obsessed with avenging his wife's brutal, savage beating and rape.

South Philly

The van pulled up and parked behind a large building near 18th Street. Outside waiting was Johnny Marino and his partner Chow-men. Three of their armed bodyguards stood close by. Terry and Magic got out of the van and opened a sliding door. Magic reached in and grabbed the large, black body bag from the van. They dragged the bag over to Johnny and Chow and dropped it at their feet.

"Here is your wanted man," Terry said, as he took a step back. Johnny unzipped the bag and looked inside. After seeing the three holes in Vance's head, he smiled and nodded.

"Are you the person that called us a few weeks ago?" Chow asked.

"Here's your body," Terry said, ignoring the question.

Chow looked over at one of his Triad goons and said, "Bring it over."

The man calmly walked over carrying a large briefcase. He then passed it to Terry. Inside the briefcase was $1.5 Million dollars, the street ransom for Vance's head. There were no handshakes or hugs, just total silence. Johnny Marino and Chow-men watched as Terry and Magic walked back to the van and got inside. A few moments later, the van was backing up and disappearing into the darkness of the night.

"Why didn't you kill them?" Johnny asked.

"Because I looked in his eyes and I saw a man of loyalty, hiding behind so much pain. Today was not his day to die."

Chapter 69
North Philly

Inside the darkness of the cemetery, King stood back watching as members of Vance's crew were all being thrown into large burial plots. King had given his men the word to execute a major sweep of all Vance's street soldiers, workers, and enforcers. Twelve men had been kidnapped at gunpoint and driven to the private cemetery. King had four men placed in each of the large plots. They had all been stripped naked. King looked down into one of the graves and said, "This is what happens when you work for a rat."

Biggie, Gotti, Marvin, and Zeta stood there holding small cans of gasoline. As the men started to scream out for their lives, they started to pour the gasoline on their naked bodies. Every time one tried to climb out of the grave he fell down. The ten-foot grave was too deep to climb out of. After lighting one of their shirts on fire King tossed it into one of the graves and watched as it woofed in flames. Then Biggie and Zeta did the same thing to the other plots.

Screams of the twelve men that were burning alive filled the dark sky. King stood back and watched the naked men burn to death. When all twelve of the men were dead, King had one of his men use a small front-end loader to fill each grave with dirt. An hour later, each grave was filled with dirt, leaving no clues of the twelve bodies behind.

"His entire crew is gone," Zeta said, as they all walked out of the cemetery.

"There are still a few more. We still need to get to Vance, Terry and the Russian," King replied.

"And we will," Biggie said.

"Me and Marvin still got some business to take care of," Gotti said, walking over to the car.

"Call me when you're done," King told him before he and Marvin drove off.

"How is Queen doing on her vacation?" Biggie asked King.

"We talked earlier and she really sounds upbeat. She will be back soon, hopefully back to her old self," King said, as they all got back into the Suburban.

Chapter 70
One Hour Later
Northeast Philly

JoAnn Morgan had been crying all day long. She still had yet to hear a single word from Vance. At the same time, the Feds were out on the streets of Philly searching for their number one informant. As JoAnn lay in bed under the covers, she heard a strange sound coming from downstairs.

"Baby is that you?" she yelled out.

With excitement in her voice, JoAnn quickly jumped from the bed and ran out of the bedroom. Her eyes lit up in fear when she saw the two masked men standing there holding guns with infrared beams attached. Without hesitation, the two men started firing their guns into JoAnn's unprotected flesh. They watched as her body dropped hard on the floor. Walking over JoAnn's dead body, they started to ransack the entire house.

Moments later, Gotti and Marvin were back inside the Impala headed towards the Boulevard. Like so many others JoAnn Morgan had been murdered for being guilty by association.

"That's the price you pay for loving a snitch," Gotti said as they drove on.

Early the Next Morning

King couldn't believe his eyes as he read the front page of the *Philadelphia Inquirer*. The headline read, "Drug Kingpin Found Dead in South Philly."

King sat back reading the article in complete shock. Someone had gotten to Vance before he could. He was a little disappointed, but at the same time, he was content. His long-time enemy was now dead, and most of his crew had been wiped out. But as long as there were others King knew that he had to stay sharp and even more focused. So many enemies were still out there, all gunning for the crown.

West Philly

"I have to disappear for a while. I'm sure I'm next on the FBI list," Victor told Terry and Magic.

They watched as Victor got into a car.

"You know how to reach me if you guys need me," he said, before leaving.

After Victor drove away Terry and Magic got into a car headed for New York City.

"Are you ready for this?" Magic asked.

"Excited, Terry said, "I was born ready."

Chapter 71
Los Angeles, CA

Queen was stunned by the article she read on her laptop. The news of her father's tragic death had her more confused than sad. The thought of both her parents being dead had touched her soul, but she felt no sorrow at all for Vance's death. He had been dead to her for as long as she could remember.

The question that everyone wanted to know was who killed him? After closing her laptop, Queen put on her sweat suit and Nikes and went for a walk to clear all of the thoughts that were running through her head.

Downtown Philly

Candice Shaw's phone had been ringing off the hook all morning. Everyone wanted to know about the Vance Lewis' murder and the twelve missing members in his drug organization. Seeing a call coming in from the FBI Director Candice quickly answered.

"Hello Director, how can I help you?"

"Ms. Shaw, does your office have any information on the murder of Vance Lewis?" he asked desperately. Candice gave a long sigh and said, "I'm sorry, I can't help you with that sir, Vance Lewis's murder is currently being investigated by the Philadelphia Homicide Division. Until we find some concrete evidence with his case, everything has to remain confidential. It's no longer an FBI case, it's a Philadelphia Police case, and we will do everything in our power to get to the bottom of this and the other murder."

"What other murder?" the Director asked frustratingly.

"Oh, you didn't hear about JoAnn Morgan?" she said.

"No, what's wrong with JoAnn?"

"She's dead too. Last night she was shot numerous times at her Northeast home. My detectives are at the house now combing through everything. We already found out that she and Vance were in a relationship and that Ms. Morgan was an associate of the FBI."

"We need to talk as soon as possible!" The Director said. "I need you to shut the entire investigation down!" he yelled.

"Sorry sir, I can't do that. This entire case is under Philadelphia jurisdiction," Candice said before ending the call.

With a smile on her face, Candice crossed her arms and shook her head.

"What the hell is going on?" she asked herself.

Chapter 72
Bronx, NY

Magic parked the car and he and Terry both got out. They stood outside a bodega on the corner of 194th & Webster. A short, chubby Dominican man walked out of the store and said, "You Terry?"

"Yeah, I'm here for Felix."

"Follow me, holmes," the man said.

Terry and Magic followed the man into the store and straight to the back. They then walked up a flight of stairs and into a small room. Inside the room, a tall, handsome Dominican man with curly hair and a goatee was sitting in a chair waiting for them.

"My name is Felix," the man said, shaking both of their hands. The short Dominican man stood against the wall and didn't say a word.

My cousin Rosa told me a lot of good things about you. We have been waiting for a while now."

"I just got Rosa's letter not too long ago and in it she gave me this address and your name," Terry said.

"Yes, I received a letter as well," Felix replied. "I heard about all your troubles in Philly and the situation with Vance," Felix continued, shaking his head in disappointment. "What a waste. We recently found out that Vance was responsible for my cousin Tito and Paco's Federal arrest. There's a five-million-dollar ransom on his head."

"Save your money, Vance is dead," Terry said.
Felix smiled and nodded his head. No more words needed to be said about the matter.

"Well, I'm here for you to finish what you started with my cousin Rosa. We are now behind you, so anything you need from us to help with your war against King you will have," Felix said, confidently.

"So, what do you know about King?" Terry asked.

"Yes, every major drug boss on the East Coast knows about King. He is the cousin of a legend and is the current boss in Philly. We need you to run Philly. We need our man in that position. Philly is a major market, and right now King is in our way." Felix said.

"And what about Rosa?"

"She was finally transferred to a female prison in West Virginia. Don't worry; she will be just fine," Felix smiled. "So, are you in, Terry?"

With a big smile he said, "Yes, I'm all the way in."

As Terry and Felix discussed business, Magic stood in awe of the entire situation. He was no longer a small-time hustler or one of Vance's middlemen or muscle. He was Terry's Second in Command, his right-hand man. After the meeting ended Felix and his friend watched as Terry and Magic got back into their car and drove off.

"He is just the man we needed to take over Philly," Felix said. "He is a man of loyalty," he added.

Felix Gonzalez was a top member of the Dominican Cartel. His father Julio Gonzalez was one of the most powerful drug bosses in the world. He had partners with top Mexican and Colombian cartels. With over a billion dollars in wealth and assets Julio Gonzalez was a force to be reckoned with, and when it came to his only child, Felix, there was nothing he wouldn't do for him.

Three Weeks Later

Queen was so happy to finally get back home. When King saw her, he couldn't believe his eyes. Queen had looked better than she had ever looked before. Her body was in tip top shape, and all her scars and injuries had healed. There was a glow in her eyes and a powerful, positive aura. Her face had healed so well that it was almost impossible to tell that she had any surgeries at all. Even Gary had changed in his appearance. He now looked like a strong, healthy man without a problem in the world.

That night while lying in bed naked Queen kissed all over King's body.

"I'm not ready for sex yet babe but lay back so I can please you in another way," Queen told him.

"Are you sure, I can wait."

"No, I miss my dick and tonight I'm going to show you how badly," Queen said, pushing King back on the large, king sized bed. With his eyes closed, King lay there while Queen got situated between his legs and started to suck his hard dick with all the pleasure she could muster. King was on cloud nine, and Queen didn't hold back. Her tongue took complete control.

"I miss my dick," she said.

Chapter 73
One Month Later
Baltimore, MD

Gary was parked across the street from the small row house. Sitting right beside him was Queen. In all seriousness, Queen didn't say a word as she suddenly opened the door and stepped out of the car.

She calmly walked across the street and approached the front door. She knocked twice and waited. The door opened and Sofie stood there frozen in fear. It was like she had seen a ghost from her past. Queen pulled her hand from her pocket holding a loaded .380 pistol. She reached out and grabbed Sofie's throat, then closed the door behind them. She forced Sofie into the living room where a small, infant boy was crying in his crib.

"Please don't kill my baby!" Sofie cried out.

"Your baby! Who is the father?" Queen snapped. Sofie stood there in total terror. She had never been more scared in all her life.

"Bitch I'm going to ask you again, who is the motherfucking father?"

"He's King's son. I never got the abortion. I just couldn't do it!" Sofie cried.

"Bitch, are you serious? Are you fucking crazy! You had my husband's child?"

"I'm sorry Queen! I couldn't allow myself to get rid of him. He is a part of me as well. I didn't have anyone, and you left me for King."

Queen stood there boiling with anger. She had never felt so much hatred or betrayal. She aimed the gun at Sofie's head and unloaded half of her clip. Sofie fell to the floor, dying where she stood. Queen then rushed upstairs and found Sofie's sister in the shower. She shot her twice and watched as her body slumped in the tub and her blood ran down the drain.

Back downstairs Queen stood over the crying baby boy. He was almost the spitting image of his father. With tears rolling from her eyes Queen aimed the gun at the baby's head. But her soul wouldn't allow her to go through with it. Seeing the child was like looking into the eyes of the only man she had ever loved. Queen put the gun away and picked up the baby. After wrapping him in a thick blanket she calmly walked out the front door and over to the waiting car.

Brighton Beach, Brooklyn New York

Victor had left Philly and came to New York where he knew it was safer. Brighton Beach was home to one of the largest Russian populations on the East Coast, and here, Victor was surrounded by many friends from the old country. He needed this new environment to rest and get his mind right. He had been devastated by his sister's death and all the recent events that had taken place in Philly.

So for the time being, Victor rented a room from a cousin and stayed under the radar. Victor made a personal promise to return to Philly in a year. He would not rest until King and everyone in his organization were dead. It was vengeance that kept him alive.

Chapter 74
Later that Evening
Wynnewood, PA

When Queen walked into her lavish home King was upstairs in the bedroom waiting for her. With the sleeping baby in her arms, she walked up the steps. A flow of tears ran down her face. When Queen entered the master bedroom, King stood there speechless.

"What's going on?" he asked, seeing her crying and holding a newborn child in her arms.

"What's going on Queen? Talk to me," King said. "Whose baby is that?"

Queen laid the baby on the bed then walked over to King. She tearfully stared into his confused eyes and said, "He's your son!!"

"What?" King replied.

"He's your son, King!" Queen cried out.

Together they sat down on the edge of the bed and Queen told King the entire story about Sofie and what she had done. When she finished her story, King was dumbfounded, with a look of total surprise plastered on his face.

"So now what? What are we going to do?" King asked. Queen looked deep into King's eyes and said, "We are gonna raise our son." Then she reached out and gave him a reassuring hug.

Calvary Cemetery, Conshohocken, PA

Terry stood a few feet away from Vance Lewis' tombstone.

"How could you, Vance?" he said. "How could you go against everything we stood for?"

Terry walked closer to the tombstone and fell to his knees.

"You were like a father to me and my brother. We believed in you!"

Terry stood up and said, "Don't worry, they might have won the battle, but the war is still undecided. I'm putting my new team together, and no rats are allowed," he laughed. "I'm gonna win this war with King, and I don't need the Feds to help me. I'm gonna win it with heart, muscle, and power."

Terry then turned on a heel and walked over to the Range Rover where Magic was waiting inside.

"You good now?" he asked.

"No, but I will be," Terry replied.

As Magic slowly pulled out of the cemetery, Terry said, "Now, let the real games begin."

COMING 2018

JIMMY DASAINT

PRESENTS:

KING III

"THE GAME OF DEATH"

*****NOW AVAILABLE*****

COMING SOON

WE SHIP TO PRISONS

BLACK SCARFACE

BLACK SCARFACE II

BLACK SCARFACE III

BLACK SCARFACE IV

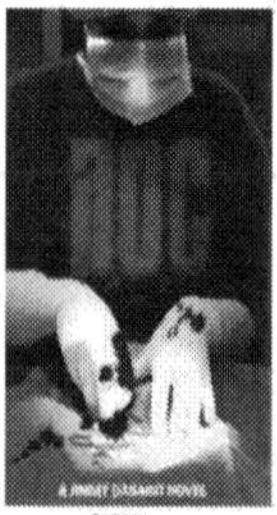

DOC

KING

KING 2

KILLADELPHIA

ON EVERYTHING I LOVE

MONEY DESIRES & REGRETS

WHAT EVERY WOMAN WANTS

YOUNG RICH & DANGEROUS

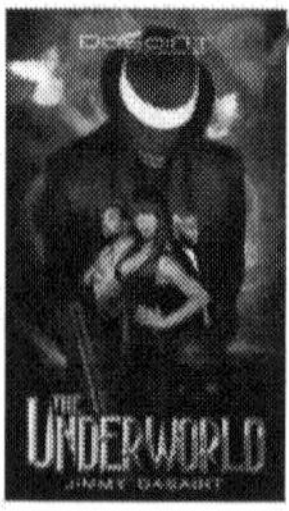

THE UNDERWORLD

A ROSE AMONG THORNS

A ROSE AMONG THORNS 2

SEX SLAVE

WE SHIP TO PRISONS

AIN'T NO SUNSHINE

WHO

THE DARKEST CORNER

HOTTEST SUMMER EVER

BLACK GOTTI

CONTRACT KILLER

THE 21 LESSONS OF LIFE

COMING SOON

SOSA

THE CREW

THE RISE OF A DYNASTY

DaSaint ENTERTAINMENT

WE SHIP TO PRISONS

DASAINT ENTERTAINMENT SPECIALS ✓

Orders being shipped to a **PRISON FACILITY ONLY**, qualify for the 3 for $30 Special! The books marked with a red checkmark can be purchased. This special **does not** include the BLACK SCARFACE Series, DOC, KING titles, or The 21 Lessons of Life. The flat rate shipping for these items are $8.00.

DASAINT ENTERTAINMENT REFUND POLICY

No Refunds Will Be Processed. All Sales Are Final!

If you submit the wrong address for any order or forget an inmate identification number, you must pay for shipping cost again, for those books to be redelivered.

If your item is returned to us by a prions facility, for any reason, you must pay to have those items shipped to another address. Return merchandize are held for ninety days. If they are not claimed by then, they will not be shipped out.

DASAINT ENTERTAINMENT ORDER FORM
Please visit www.dasaintentertainment.com to place online orders.

You can also fill out this form and send it to:
DASAINT ENTERTAINMENT
PO BOX 97
BALA CYNWYD, PA 19004

TITLE	PRICE	QTY
BLACK SCARFACE	$15.00	_____
BLACK SCARFACE II	$15.00	_____
BLACK SCARFACE III	$15.00	_____
BLACK SCARFACE IV	$15.00	_____
DOC	$15.00	_____
KING	$15.00	_____
KING 2	$15.00	_____
KILLADELPHIA	$15.00	_____
ON EVERYTHING I LOVE	$15.00	_____
MONEY DESIRES & REGRETS	$15.00	_____
WHAT EVERY WOMAN WANTS	$15.00	_____
YOUNG RICH & DANGEROUS	$15.00	_____
THE UNDERWORLD	$15.00	_____
A ROSE AMONG THORNS	$15.00	_____
A ROSE AMONG THORNS II	$15.00	_____
SEX SLAVE	$15.00	_____
AIN'T NO SUNSHINE	$15.00	_____
WHO	$15.00	_____
THE DARKEST CORNER	$15.00	_____
HOTTEST SUMMER EVER	$15.00	_____
BLACK GOTTI	$15.00	_____
CONTRACT KILLER	$15.00	_____
THE 21 LESSONS OF LIFE	$12.99	_____

WE SHIP TO PRISONS

Make Money Orders payable to:
DASAINT ENTERTAINMENT (NO CHECKS ACCEPTED)

NAME: ____

ADDRESS: ____

____

CITY: ____________________________ STATE: _____ ZIP: _________

PHONE: ________________________ EMAIL: ____________________

PRISON ID NUMBER ______________________

$3.00 per item for Shipping and Handling
($4.95 per item for Expedited Shipping)

DASAINT ENTERTAINMENT ORDER FORM
Please visit www.dasaintentertainment.com to place online orders.

You can also fill out this form and send it to:
DASAINT ENTERTAINMENT
PO BOX 97
BALA CYNWYD, PA 19004

TITLE	PRICE	QTY
BLACK SCARFACE	$15.00	_____
BLACK SCARFACE II	$15.00	_____
BLACK SCARFACE III	$15.00	_____
BLACK SCARFACE IV	$15.00	_____
DOC	$15.00	_____
KING	$15.00	_____
KING 2	$15.00	_____
KILLADELPHIA	$15.00	_____
ON EVERYTHING I LOVE	$15.00	_____
MONEY DESIRES & REGRETS	$15.00	_____
WHAT EVERY WOMAN WANTS	$15.00	_____
YOUNG RICH & DANGEROUS	$15.00	_____
THE UNDERWORLD	$15.00	_____
A ROSE AMONG THORNS	$15.00	_____
A ROSE AMONG THORNS II	$15.00	_____
SEX SLAVE	$15.00	_____
AIN'T NO SUNSHINE	$15.00	_____
WHO	$15.00	_____
THE DARKEST CORNER	$15.00	_____
HOTTEST SUMMER EVER	$15.00	_____
BLACK GOTTI	$15.00	_____
CONTRACT KILLER	$15.00	_____
THE 21 LESSONS OF LIFE	$12.99	_____

WE SHIP TO PRISONS

Make Money Orders payable to:
DASAINT ENTERTAINMENT (NO CHECKS ACCEPTED)

NAME: ____

ADDRESS: ____

____

CITY: ______________________ STATE: _____ ZIP: _________

PHONE: ____________________ EMAIL: ____________________

PRISON ID NUMBER ____________________

$3.00 per item for Shipping and Handling
($4.95 per item for Expedited Shipping)

Duplicate Order Form

Made in the USA
Columbia, SC
15 November 2021

48999376R00104